For Keith

SCARLET RIBBONS

MARK L. FOWLER

Mark

For Linda Mayne

CHAPTER ONE

The boy screamed. He couldn't move; his feet rooted to the ground in terror. And then the spell broke, and he was in motion, his little legs firing away like pistons, running for his life, the hut receding behind him, his mother charging across the grass from the opposite direction.

Slow motion seconds ticked as the world stood still, and then all sound rushed back in, like an atomic blast, reality returning to full speed, the terrified boy shaking from head to toe, standing cradled in his mother's arms as she gripped him tightly.

"Jack! Oh my God, what is it?"

It had been a beautiful spring afternoon at the lido, Jack's fifth birthday; a picnic for the boy, his mum, and Jean, his new baby sister. The family had planned to go out later, an evening at the circus when dad got home from work; a perfect day.

The colour had drained completely from the little boy's face, turning him into a ghost. His mother, still holding onto her son, was scanning the park in every direction, seeing nothing, and asking him again, "What is it, my darling, what's the matter?"

With a trembling hand Jack pointed towards the old park keeper's hut.

A minute earlier he had set off, leaving his family behind, following the flight path of his toy aeroplane. Then a gust of wind had lifted the new glider and carried it beyond where the family were enjoying their picnic, and Jack had gone scampering after it, hooting with delight as it dipped and rose again, travelling even beyond the old hut that stood just ahead of the rusted railings.

Tears were flowing down his face and dripping from his chin.

"What is it, Jack? What have you seen?"

Gulping to get his breath, he struggled to get his words out.

"It's a woman, mummy."

His mother frowned, looking back to where her son was pointing.

"A woman?" she said.

"Yes ... but she hasn't got a face."

CHAPTER TWO

DCI Tyler stood erect and silent, observing the scene with an air of detachment.

The dead woman had been discovered behind the park keeper's hut, in the narrow stretch between the back of the derelict building and the railings that ran parallel. The hedges beyond, on the adjacent footpath, were thick enough to obscure the corpse from anyone passing on that side, and so it had been the flight path of a little boy's toy glider that had led to the gruesome discovery.

Tyler observed that the woman had platinum blonde hair, and she was wearing a low-cut pink t-shirt with the word 'Glamour' printed across the front of it in sparkly silver print. She was also wearing a short black skirt and high heel shoes. Her hair was streaked and matted with blood from the deep facial wounds that she had sustained, and her shirt was soaked through with what had gushed out from the gash across her throat.

The area of the lido around her had been marked off with police tape, as the crime investigation unit began its task of searching for evidence. DS Mills was crossing the police line and he took his place next to the DCI. "Jesus!" he said, looking on.

Tyler didn't respond.

The face, or what little remained of it, had been slashed to ribbons, and the throat cut through. "*Jesus Christ,*" said Mills.

Tyler looked at his colleague, but neither of the detectives said anything, both seemingly haunted back into silence by what lay on the ground in front of them.

"A little boy found her," said Tyler at last. "He was enjoying a birthday picnic in the park with his family."

Mills shook his head. "This is one birthday the poor little sod won't forget," he said.

"Evidence of recent sexual activity, but not necessarily of sexual assault," said Tyler, as though thinking aloud.

Mills waited for more from the DCI. But for the moment nothing was forthcoming. He turned his back on the scene and took a few deep breaths. "Anyone reported missing that might ..?"

"Not yet," said Tyler. "Come on, let's make tracks and let these good people get on with their work."

Mills glanced one last time at the mutilated corpse before following Tyler in the direction of the main car park.

CHAPTER THREE

Late that evening Mills was sitting up in bed when his wife came into the bedroom.

"You alright, Danny?" she said.

"I've had better days."

"Want to talk about it?"

She got undressed and slipped in beside him. "It's that woman – the one on the news? The woman found at the lido?"

"That's the one."

"I heard it on the radio. Not that they're saying much."

"There isn't much to say. We don't know a lot, not yet. We're waiting for someone to come forward and at least report the poor girl missing. But they'll have a job identifying her."

"That bad?"

"Practically cut the poor thing's face off."

"Who would do a thing like that?"

"That's what we're hoping to find out."

His wife shuddered. "Sometimes ... I don't know how you can do this job." She took hold of his hand. "I'm proud of you all the same. Are you working with Jim Tyler?"

Mills nodded.

"How's he doing these days?"

"It's shook him up. He'd never let on, of course, you know what he's like."

"It's bound to have an effect, though, seeing a thing like that. It's enough to shake anyone." She kissed the side of her husband's face. "Can I get you anything?"

"A ten-pint party pack, and then I might have a chance of sleeping tonight," he said.

"Let's hope Jim's not thinking along those lines."

"Don't even go there. He's likely out running."

"If that's how he copes with it, love, it's better than the alternatives. He still goes out on his epics?"

"Every time he gets the urge to drink or to punch someone," said Mills. "Running and work, I swear they're the only things keeping him sane."

"If this line of work helps keep him sane ... then God help him!" She thought for a moment. "What happened with that officer he was seeing?"

"They've transferred her down to London. And you know what Jim thinks about that place."

Tyler had arrived in the city of Stoke on Trent as an exile from the capital after assaulting a senior officer. He'd vowed to never set foot there again, on any account, or to touch another drink. He'd made no similar vows when it came to standing up to bullies, regardless of their rank.

"So she's having to make the journey back to Stoke if she wishes to see him?"

Mills shrugged.

"You mean, you haven't asked? What are you men like?"

"You know what *he's* like. He doesn't talk about personal stuff, his feelings and all that. Getting blood out of a stone would be easy compared -"

"But you could at least try. He might want to talk about it, Danny."

"And he might not. I've had my head chewed off too many times for poking my nose in where it doesn't belong. Anyway, if you don't mind, I'm going to try and catch an hour."

She switched out the light and kissed him. "Goodnight Danny."

It was long after the light went out; Mills listening to the sound of soft snoring coming from the other side of the bed, but feeling far from sleep. All he could see in the darkness, whether he closed his eyes or opened them, was the grim remains of the faceless woman.

CHAPTER FOUR

Following a briefing conducted in the presence of Chief Superintendent Berkins, Tyler and Mills went through the preliminary findings from forensics.

The woman, most likely in her late teens or early twenties, had been killed within twenty four hours of being found, and probably during the night prior to her discovery, the lido being well used during the day time. She had died as a consequence of the wound to her throat, the subsequent wounding to her face appearing to have been conducted post mortem. There was little evidence of a significant struggle having taken place, no material found under her finger nails and no traces of blood at the scene that did not match her type. It was confirmed that she had indeed engaged in sexual activity recently, but there was nothing to suggest that this had not been consensual.

A public appeal for information had gone out, in the hope that someone might realise that a loved one was missing. The time wasters were having field day, as they generally did under such circumstances. But later that day a call came in that sounded like it could be genuine.

"Sir, we've got Christine Rayworth downstairs," said Mills. He'd taken the call from his desk in the CID office, relaying the information to Tyler who was at that moment sitting opposite him. "She rang in earlier, but didn't wish to give her contact details; preferred to pay us a visit."

"Who is she?"

"All she's said so far is that her colleague hasn't shown up for work. She's worried about her, and has a bad feeling she might be the victim."

The detectives headed down the staircase and entered one of the interview rooms, where a young woman sat waiting. She looked up and offered a timid smile.

Tyler scrutinised the woman: attractive, in a rough sort of way, he thought; early twenties, at a guess, with raven black hair cut short, accentuating bloodless skin and piercing pale blue eyes. She confirmed her name, and that her missing colleague was Stacey Trent.

"When did you last see Stacey?" he asked her.

"We worked the Sunday shift."

"What time was that?"

"It was a quiet night. We knocked off early. We left around midnight."

"You mentioned that she failed to turn up for her next shift. When would that have been?"

"Yesterday afternoon. She doesn't work Mondays, not Monday evenings at least. We kick in around two or three and stay until closing."

"You've tried to contact her?"

"Of course I have. I'm not stupid. I went to her flat after my shift, and I went round again this morning. I've never known Stacey miss a shift before and I'm worried about her."

"What is it that you both do?" asked Mills.

The woman hesitated and Tyler appeared to nod subtly as though his suspicions had been confirmed.

"We work in the ... you know ... *the trade*."

"I see," said Tyler.

"This is confidential, right?"

13

Mills looked about to say something, and then retreated; an unbalanced coin at last making the drop.

"Where are you based?" asked Tyler.

While Rayworth spoke he scribbled down some notes:

Stacey Trent, Flat 14, Smithpool Street, Heron Cross. Works at West End Girls, *Munster Gardens, West End, Stoke; and* The Sweet Box, *Waterloo Road, Burslem. Platinum blonde, cut short, approximately five six in height and nine and a half stone in weight; a small tattoo at the base of her spine - a tiger about to strike.*

That last detail was the clincher. Tyler said, "Christine, do you know of anyone who might wish to harm Stacey?"

CHAPTER FIVE

"It's her isn't it?" Rayworth folded forward, her hands over her face. "Her flat's across from the lido. Some bastard's attacked her, some bastard's killed Stacey."

According to Rayworth her colleague's last shift had been at *West End Girls* - and after they finished the two women had gone their separate ways. Rayworth lived in Stoke, no more than half a mile from work, and so had made the journey home on foot. Stacey, she said, usually called a taxi and generally used City Cabs.

The two detectives were back in the CID office, Mills making a brew. "Early finish for that game," he said handing a mug of tea to Tyler. "I thought they'd be at it until the early hours."

"Made a close study of the 'game', have you?"

"I watch all of the cop shows on the telly," said Mills. "They're a mine of information. Particularly the American ones," he added, his tongue pressing pointedly into the side of his cheek.

"So that's the secret of how you rose to Detective Sergeant." Tyler took a sip of his drink and winced. "You most certainly didn't get there through your tea making."

"Don't blame me. I think the milk's turning."

Tyler placed the drink to one side. "Sunday evenings are likely quiet because the punters are at home with their families for one night a week. Regular family guys you understand."

His tone was acidic and Mills knew better than to argue. Instead, he checked with City Cabs, but there had been no pick up from West End around that time on Sunday night.

Trent and Rayworth, according to the latter's account, had been the last to leave the premises. Business had been slow later into the evening and Rayworth claimed that the two girls had elected to be the ones to stick around to catch any late trade following drinking up time at the local pubs.

"Maybe she walked," said Mills. "It's only a couple of miles. The weather was fine on Sunday night."

"It's always possible. No picnic in high heels I would imagine."

"Maybe she was hoping to pick up more business along the way," said Mills, giving up with his own drink and placing it down on the desk. "I mean, if they'd had a quiet night ..."

"You *have* been watching a lot of TV," said Tyler. "Meanwhile, back in the real world - did you get a ring back yet from this Hayley Greener?"

Greener was the proprietor of *West End Girls*, and Rayworth had given the detectives her business and private contact numbers.

"I'll try her again."

The line connected. When the call ended, Mills said, "She's at the premises now."

Tyler was on his feet. "Come on," he said, "let's further our education."

They made their way out to the car park, and as Mills took his place behind the wheel and negotiated his way into the traffic Tyler said, "What did you make of Rayworth?"

"In what sense, sir?"

"It's an open question. Your observations?"

Mills thought for a minute. Tyler rarely made small talk, but if he was getting at something, the DS was at a loss as to what that might be.

16

The traffic cleared as they headed towards Stoke but still Mills had made no headway on the DCI's question. "In your own time," prompted Tyler as Mills navigated the one-way system into the town centre.

"I'd have to say that Rayworth was cut up, sir."

"Unfortunate expression, under the circumstances, don't you think."

"Sorry sir. I didn't mean to -"

"I know you didn't. But go on."

"Well, I'd say that she came in here hoping that her worries that her colleague was the dead woman would be proved wrong. I'd say that she knew that detail about the tattoo would call it either way, and from our reaction she knew the score."

Mills turned into London Road and headed back out of the town centre towards the West End.

Tyler nodded. "Very good," he said.

Mills glanced across for a clue as to what Tyler might be getting at, but the DCI's poker face was holding firm.

A few hundred yards up the road the DS indicated right and promptly turned into Munster Gardens. To the immediate right stood half a dozen business properties, with *West End Girls* positioned at the far end of the row. The detectives got out of the car.

"I assume that Munster Gardens is named in dedication to the weeds growing through the pavement."

"I believe so," said Mills.

Tyler gave him a look. "Rumours of the death of sarcasm have been wildly exaggerated."

"I'm pleased to hear that, sir."

The sign looked hand written and had been nailed above a door that someone had tried to kick through.

17

"Kindly do the honours," said Tyler.

Mills knocked on the door, and after a few moments it was opened by a large woman who looked to be settling into her early sixties with an accompanying air of resignation. She gestured to the detectives to enter.

The property had a tardic quality, appearing to expand on the inside from its somewhat deceptively cosy exterior. The woman led the detectives through a long hallway, with closed doors flanking on both sides, before arriving at an office towards the rear of the building. She flopped down behind a desk and gestured to the detectives to likewise take a seat.

"Hayley Greener," she said. "I own *West End Girls* and we offer a valuable service to our community. Our workers earn a reasonable rate of pay and their health and well being is valued here. It is a darned sight safer working at *West End Girls* than plying one's trade out on the streets of this city and I have the statistics to prove it."

The woman looked defiantly from one detective to the other, as though to challenge any contradiction to her mission statement.

Mills thought she looked as though she might launch a complaint against them for harassment at any moment.

"We understand that you employ a worker by the name of Stacey Trent," said Tyler.

"That's correct. She's worked for me for almost twelve months."

"She was working here on Sunday?"

"Her shift ended at midnight."

"Were you on the premises on Sunday?"

"I was not. Actually, on Sunday evening I was at our other business site." Tyler waited, all the time looking

18

at her questioningly. "That would be *The Sweet Box*, in Burslem. On Waterloo Road. We had a busy evening and I was there until well after two on Monday morning."

It briefly crossed Mills' mind that family time was spent differently in the north of the city, though he kept the observation to himself. Despite being a south east of the city Longton boy through and through, and raised on the inner hub's inverted snobbery, he always strived to guard against the prejudicial attitudes that still fed the city's north/south divide. And anyway, he had to concede that while home was home, there wasn't much to choose between north and south when it came to identifying the top awards for local squalor.

Mills was back in the room, aware that Tyler had asked another question.

"... Stacey worked both premises as part of the rota. It operates partly as a safety mechanism to keep the girls safe. We occasionally do get clients who fixate on one of our staff, and so we ensure that they are less available, for that reason."

"You don't have any clients who use both of your premises?" asked Mills.

He instantly felt the weight of two pairs of eyes scrutinising him, suggesting he had asked either the vital question that would lead to the cracking of the case, or else had made a complete fool of himself. He couldn't work out which.

"That has never happened, as far as I'm aware," said Greener. "Our customers tend to prefer to use their local service providers exclusively."

"I see," said Mills. He almost added, 'Commendable', but withdrew the urge in the nick of time.

19

The room fell silent. Then Greener sighed, heavily. "It is Stacey, isn't it? Christine called me, said it was looking that way. Some savage bastard's killed her."

"Have any of your clients made threats against her, or against any of her colleagues?" asked Tyler.

"We have the occasional issue," said Greener. "Nothing serious enough to merit a call to you lot; but you get the odd creep come in from time to time. I run a tight ship, here and at *The Sweet Box*, and we have a zero tolerance policy. Any funny business and it's a lifetime ban, no ifs and buts, you're out! Naturally, we've closed both premises today, as a mark of respect."

She looked at the detectives, and appeared surprised not to receive a round of applause for her sensitive and respectful actions.

"You mentioned having occasional issues," said Tyler.

"I'm talking about the Three Amigos," said Greener. She laughed. "For the uninitiated, that would be Stan, Roy and Ted. Creeps, alright, but I don't see them killing anyone; still, you never know, and I suppose that's your job anyway, not mine."

"The Three Amigos?" said Tyler.

"I don't have full names and addresses, if that's what you're after. We offer a discreet service here. I imagine you can understand that?"

There was something in the way she looked at Mills as she said that, causing him a mild blush; as though he was being accused of something, of being a man, perhaps.

"Stan visits our Burslem site, and has done for years. Then he went through a phase of getting a bit rough with the girls."

"But your zero policy sorted him out?" said Tyler.

Greener's eyes seemed to glow with latent hostility. "He was given a warning, actually. It was out of character, and so we granted him another chance. We haven't had any problems since."

"And how long ago was this?"

"A few weeks now I should think."

"A month?"

"Couple of weeks certainly."

Tyler drew a long and silent breath. "What day does he attend *The Sweet Box*?"

"I can check the log. You can set your watch and calendar by some of our regulars. I'm thinking late Friday afternoon, but I'll check."

"I would appreciate that," said Tyler. "How rough was he getting with the girls?"

Greener finished checking. "Yes, Fridays, that's his day. Oh, nothing too heavy, you understand; bit of a slap here and there, but we told him straight: if that's what you're into these days, Stan, you pay the going rate or you take your business elsewhere. I mean, he must be eighty if he's a day. I don't think there's any harm to him. Look, I don't want you lot coming in whenever you please and scaring off all our punters ..." Greener cleared her throat, and when she spoke again she had adopted a gentler tone. "Of course, you need to find out who did this thing. But I'm sure you can be sensitive about it ... and discreet."

She seemed to look again at Mills, and the DS felt the return of the earlier blush warming his cheeks and the back of his neck.

"You also mentioned Roy and Ted," said Tyler.

"Ah, Roy and Ted: no spring chickens either. But I can go further for you there. A couple of right

21

characters they are and both of them living practically on our doorstep. Roy Hately - he's been coming in for a year or more. They all know Roy!

"And as for Ted ..."

CHAPTER SIX

Ted Freely lived around the corner from *West End Girls*, on Gladstone Avenue, in a small detached property with a large collection of garden gnomes eccentrically populating a pristine front lawn. He was a slight, bald headed man in his early seventies, with peevish eyes magnified behind the thick lenses of his black-rimmed spectacles. Whilst the eyes might have betrayed a peevish personality lurking behind them, his manner appeared at odds with this, and he welcomed the detectives warmly across the threshold.

"Now, what can I ... *do you for* today?" he said, trying hard to contain the laughter that he appeared to be struggling to contain. "Sorry, just my little joke, you understand."

Mills raised the topic of *West End Girls*, and Freely clasped his hands together and adopted a mock-serious expression. "Bang the cuffs on," he said. "My little secret is out!"

Tyler glanced across at Mills, and then asked Freely if he was familiar with Stacey. Freely didn't attempt to deny that he was very familiar with the woman indeed. "One of my favourites," he said, licking at his lips. "Oh, yes indeed! I've been bitten by that tiger of hers more than once, I can tell you! But once bitten twice shy, as they say."

Mills looked baffled, and Freely chose to clarify the situation by letting out a roar of laughter.

"I must stop it," he said. "All of this jovial levity when there's police officers around. It is most unseemly and it has to stop. I don't mean any harm, of course, and the girls all know me. They know old Ted and they humour me. I never married, but that doesn't mean I don't like women. It just means that I never found one that I wanted to spend the day with, if you see what I mean."

A serious look came over Ted Freely, and Mills wondered if this wasn't the prelude to another of the man's jokes.

"I don't mean any harm, really I don't. Have they been complaining about me? I know I go a bit far sometimes, but they only have to say if it upsets them. I like my little games, you see. It's just old Ted, that's all it is. Ted likes to play, that's all there is to it: Old Ted and his little games."

*

Roy Hately was similarly in his early seventies and lived in the house at the far end of Munster Terrace, only yards up the road from *West End Girls*. When he opened his front door to find two detectives on his doorstep, he appeared overjoyed at the prospect of welcoming in visitors to his home.

He showed them through the filthy hallway to an equally filthy living room.

"So, to what do I owe the pleasure, gentlemen?"

The voice was educated, bordering on posh, thought Mills.

"We understand that you are a regular visitor to *West End Girls*," said Tyler.

The man groaned, theatrically. "I'm afraid I have to confess: guilty as charged. I hadn't realised it was a police matter. But then times change quickly these days, don't they?"

He sat down wearily, leaving the detectives standing.

"You see, I do try to fight it, but I get ... well, the truth is, I do get rather lonely. I've been on my own a good while, you see. I used to pray nightly for deliverance from my loneliness, and - and I don't mean to be disrespectful or even facetious – but when *West End Girls* opened, and practically on my doorstep, well, they do say that God can move in most mysterious ways."

Mills tried to conceal a grin.

"I don't imagine that Martha, my late wife, would necessarily approve, though I hope that she might understand. It never leaves you, you know, that urge."

"Mr Hately," said Tyler; but the old man hadn't finished.

"I sometimes used to kid myself that I was only going round there for the company; to break up my evenings. I was fooling myself, naturally. Oh, that might have been part of it, and I did like to have a good chat with the girls. I paid them extra for their time, of course, that's only right and proper. I liked to tell them about my life, you see, about Martha, even, and some of them were kind enough to listen.

"Of course, it didn't stop there. They're such lovely things, those young women, and anyway it would have seemed rude not to, you know, while I was there, if you see what I mean."

"Mr Hately," Tyler tried again, "you used to ask for one of the girls in particular, is that right?"

Hately had a faraway look in his eyes, as though recalling a fond episode of intimacy. "They were all so pretty," he said, dreamily, "well, most of them were, to my eyes at least, and so young and fresh and ..."

"*Mr Hately*," said Tyler, "I believe that you used to ask to see Stacey?"

25

"Actually, they weren't all of them so gorgeous, now I think about it. Some were downright ugly; trades description ought to have been informed, and they could be quite rude, too. You'd be telling them about something quite personal, pouring your heart out, and they'd yawn right in your face and ask if you wanted a shag or not. I mean to say, manners cost nothing, and once or twice I reported them, and got myself a bit of a reputation as a trouble maker into the bargain no doubt."

"Does the name Stacey ring any bells?" cut in Mills.

"Stacey you say?" Hately shook his head. "I shouldn't think so. *Stacey*?" He thought for a few minutes. "Should the name ring a bell? Who are we talking about?"

Mills tried another tack. "Was there one of the girls who was a good listener, Mr Hately? One you liked to talk to?"

He was shaking his head. "No, that name definitely doesn't ring any bells with me. You've got the right place? I mean to say, I've probably done the rounds with most of them there, and I don't recall that name, not for the life of me I don't."

"Blonde hair," said Mills.

"A few of them have blonde hair. It's a bit of a classic, isn't it? But I don't care about anything like that; it's the personality I go for; the listening ear and the kind smile."

"A tattoo on her back?" said Mills, giving it one last try.

"What's that you say? Tattoo?" Hately gave Mills a piercing look.

"You used to ask for her by name, and she had the tattoo of a tiger on her back."

26

"I never asked for anyone called Stacey, I'd swear on my late Martha's grave. You've got it all wrong," he said.

Mills was about to speak when Hately said, "I remember that tattoo, though; that tiger just above her bottom." He smiled, and his yellow teeth poked above his tongue which was now resting on his lower lip. "I loved that tiger ... but her name wasn't Stacey, nothing like that. No, you must mean Scarlet."

CHAPTER SEVEN

The detectives once again sat opposite Hayley Greener in the back room at *West End Girls*.

"It's the name she used for the clients. Some of the girls like to adopt a persona, detach from their real identities, or whatever bullshit you might want to call it. It's up to them what name they use, or if they use any name at all."

"You said that Hately was starting to act in a creepy way," said Tyler. "Did Stacey – or Scarlet -"

"Did she talk to me about it? No, she didn't. Christine, another of our girls, she told me."

"Christine Rayworth?"

"Stacey must have talked to her about it, and she came to me. Hately was in here one day, very recently, actually, asking for 'Scarlet.' But she wasn't here on that particular day, and so Christine said she'd see to him." Mills appeared to flinch at the turn of phrase. "After the session, that's when Christine came to me and had a word. She said Hately spent all the time asking questions about Stacey."

"What kind of questions?" asked Tyler.

"Where she lived, did she work anywhere else, was she seeing anyone, that kind of thing. He was reeling them off like he was really on the case. And then the weirdest thing of all, Christine, seeing that time was getting on, took her kit off to move things forward, and what's Hately do? He only tells her to get dressed and not to be so disgusting! Said he'd never been unfaithful in his life, not when he was married, and not now he'd found his true love."

"And he was referring to Stacey?" said Mills.

"That's correct. And the next time I saw Stacey I talked to her, and she said Hately had proposed, and when she laughed about it he started to turn nasty. He told her he didn't want her sleeping with other men now that they were engaged. Said he'd keep an eye on her and make sure she didn't work here anymore. I told her that we'd stop Hately coming in, but she insisted he was harmless, and that she could handle him."

"And when was this?" asked Tyler.

"It was a couple of weeks ago when I spoke to her. I mean to say, he's an old man, I'm not saying he's dangerous, or anything like that, but you never know do you?"

"And Ted Freely," said Tyler.

"Old Ted," said Greener. "Now he's definitely a few pennies short of a pound."

"I'm curious about his 'games'."

"Aren't we all! He's another one who would ask for Stacey. Or *Tiger Girl* as he sometimes called her. We have a policy here, things you can do and things you can't. I run a respectable establishment. And when you get one who breaks the rules, it makes it harder for the others, if you get what I'm saying."

"Are we talking about Ted or Stacey breaking the rules?" asked Mills.

"The likes of Ted – he'll try his luck. He'd ask if he could play his 'games', as he called them, and of course most of the girls here would know better, put him in his place, and that would be that. But Stacey – she'd been letting him get away with murder."

Tyler's eyebrows rose at the word, though Greener appeared oblivious. She went on: "And that's the trouble, because if she lets him, you know, play his games, then there's a rumpus when the others refuse."

"And the other girls complained?" asked Mills.

"That's how I found out. I would have been having words with Stacey, I can tell you. But that's all water under the bridge now, by the sound of things. Anyway, like I say, all these are old men, and I think you'd be clutching at straws if you thought any of them was capable of, you know, what's happened. But there's another one I thought of, after you left earlier, and this guy really *does* worry me."

"Go on," said Tyler.

"He hangs around outside my other place, in Burslem. Been doing it for a few weeks now, a few of the girls have noticed him. He stands watching from across the road, watches them coming in and out of *The Sweet Box*, but he's never been inside, not to my knowledge. I've seen him myself, many a time. Tall, he is, and skinny, short ginger hair with a matching moustache. I tell you - he looks well creepy."

"When does he tend to appear outside your premises?" asked Tyler.

"Early evenings, usually around six or seven, though I'm not sure there's any particular pattern regarding which day."

"Has he approached any of your girls?"

"No, he hasn't, as far as I'm aware. He just stands there watching them as they come and go, and then he stares at the building. Bog-eyed bastard he is, and I wouldn't trust him as far as I could throw him. I really don't like the look of that man, not one little bit."

"How frequently does he turn up?" asked Mills.

"I'd say it varies. Sometimes he's there three evenings on the trot, and then we might not see him for a few days."

"And he's not been spotted here at West End?"

Greener shook her head. "Not as yet so far as I know."

The detectives made their way outside and climbed into the car, and Mills drove back to the station.

"Ted Freely's a bit of a character," he said.

"I suppose that's one word you could use. And he has no alibi for Sunday evening."

"Those games ..."

"Giving you ideas?"

"I'd be out on my ear, sir."

"Well, you'd know where to go."

"Can we cross him off the list, you reckon, along with Hately and that other one – Stan, up in Burslem?"

"I prefer to keep an open mind for the moment," said Tyler. "And let's get Christine Rayworth back in."

"Whatever you say, sir."

Mills drove on while Tyler appeared deep in thought. Mills' mind had finally drifted away from sordid speculations about Freely's games, when Tyler said, "Going back to Freely. I don't see anything there. No alibi, but no warning lights either. Hately, on the other hand ... there's an obsessive quality to that man that concerns me. A thing with Stacey, no doubt, and practically the only time he ventures out is to visit *West End Girls*. I don't know why he doesn't ask Tesco to add that service to his home delivery."

"Very droll, sir."

"I can't let you keep all the best lines."

"Fair's fair," said Mills. "You think Hately's our man, then?"

"Not particularly. But if he turns out to be, then I've got some serious explaining to do if I don't at least look into the possibility. By the way, are doing anything around six pm?"

"Now you mention it, I had my eye on a pie that's been sitting in the fridge for a couple of days."

"Your stomach ruling the roost again I notice."

"Is it that obvious?"

"Only when you're standing up or sitting down."

"I'm in between diets at the moment, sir." Mills swung onto the car park. As he got out of the car he appeared to be sucking in his abdomen, and catching Tyler's eye as he did so.

"I want to park discreetly outside *The Sweet Box* and keep an eye out for the man with the ginger hair."

"Sounds like a plot in Sherlock Holmes."

"Does it? I really wouldn't know about that."

"Yes, the one about the league of red headed gentlemen."

"I'll take your word for it."

"I had a collection of Sherlock Holmes stories one Christmas."

"And look at you now."

Mills appeared hurt by the caustic remark, but he rallied valiantly. "I thought Greener said they were closed today ... as a mark of respect?"

"But our ginger friend won't know that. We can see if he turns up, and while he's reading the sign in the window we can nab him for a word." Tyler watched Mills' mouth start to open, and he sighed. "And before you ask, I'm taking poetic licence regarding there being a sign in the window." Noting that Mills' abdomen had since expanded to its full extent once again, he added, "So, how far in-between diets are you?"

"About a month in both directions."

"Meaning that you are in the midst of a two-month eat-what-you-like dietary phase?"

Mills placed a finger up to his lips. "It's on the quiet, so not a word to the wife."

"You're saying she hasn't noticed any changes?"

"She's been a bit distracted lately. She's thinking of changing jobs and she's also been bobbing down to see her parents whenever she can. They've retired and moved homes and she's been taking the kids to see them most weekends. She's got quite a bit on her plate at the moment."

Glancing again in the direction of his colleague's sagging mid riff, Tyler said, "That's two of you with a lot on your plates, then."

"I'm a man who needs his comforts."

They made their way up to the CID room. Mills contacted Christine Rayworth and invited her to come back into the station, and then he made a drink.

"So, while the wife's been away, the pies have come out to play."

"And not only the pies," said Mills, taking a packet of chocolate digestives out of his draw. "But I think I've been rumbled."

Tyler frowned, and declined the offer when Mills pointed the packet in his direction. "There's something I don't understand, and I've enough on my mind at the moment what with murder investigations and the like."

"What is it, sir?"

"If your wife's on to you, how come you have another month of free rein in the calorie department?"

But before Mills could satisfy Tyler's curiosity on the matter, the DCI's phone rang, summoning the senior detective to the office of Chief Superintendent Berkins.

CHAPTER EIGHT

Berkins' expression was grim. "Sit down, Jim."

It wasn't exactly unprecedented in the life of Jim Tyler to be asked to sit down under the grim expression of senior management. But Berkins wasn't like any other senior that Tyler had ever come across. Most of them, in Tyler's estimation, wouldn't merit a lifejacket on board a sinking ship. Yet Berkins was one in a million.

Tyler took a seat and looked with concern at his line manager.

His run-ins with authority figures over the course of his career were near-legendary, but if there was one such figure he could abide then it was most definitely Chief Superintendent Berkins. He had never expected this exile to the City of Stoke on Trent to work out; had fully anticipated that it would mark the beginning of the end of his time as a DCI, and as a police officer come to that. But Berkins had proven to be a revelation, as had the city itself, and with DS Mills as his right hand man, he had come to count himself blessed with outrageous good fortune.

"I'll come straight to the point, Jim. I'm taking some time out."

"I see," said Tyler. "Can I ask ..?"

"Ulcers. Stress related, no doubt. But the blighters have populated my stomach and it's going to take a very sharp knife and a steady hand to dislodge them. I'm booked in next week and there's a hefty period of time set aside for recuperation. I intend to be back, but, we'll see."

Before Tyler had chance to offer his sympathies Berkins announced the other news of the day.

"They're drafting in Carstairs from south of the county."

Tyler knew the name.

"To be frank, Jim, I don't expect the two of you to hit it off. But I would urge you to make the effort. If I do eventually return, I'd sooner not inherit a war zone." Berkins sat back. "So, to business: where are we on the murder?"

Tyler brought him up to speed. It didn't take long. And when he'd finished Berkins let out a long sigh. "I understand there was no evidence of sexual assault."

"That's right."

"A hate crime, do you suppose?"

"It's a possibility. You might guess that you would have to hate someone to want to carve them up like that. The level of violence certainly indicates some strong emotions on the part of the assailant."

"It could be personal - a disgruntled boyfriend, perhaps?"

"We're still at an early stage in our investigation," said Tyler. "We don't know a lot about the victim so far. We have traced the parents, so I'm hoping to find out more later. We're also speaking again to Christine Rayworth, who seems to have known the victim quite well."

"I'm sure I'm leaving everything in capable hands, Jim. I have every confidence in you."

"Thank you, sir."

Berkins was famed throughout the department for his trademark 'nutshells' and Tyler sensed that one was imminent.

36

"I would have liked to nail this case before I went off. But my last working day is tomorrow, so even with your legendary skills, I suppose a result by then is high unlikely. I'll be keeping my eyes and ears open ..."

He broke off. It was coming. "In a nutshell, Jim ..." He broke off again, grabbing a tissue from his pocket and blotting at his face, feigning a sneeze in the process. "Sorry about that," he said, "a cold's just what I need."

But the deceit was fooling no-one in the room.

"You've every right to be on edge, Graham," said Tyler, getting up and offering his hand. "I bottle stuff up myself, God knows I'm well known for it; but it does you no good in the end. Right, then: self awareness speech over. But if you ever need an ear ..."

"Thanks, Jim," said Berkins, taking his hand. "I'll bear that in mind. Good luck with the case, and just mind how you go with Carstairs."

CHAPTER NINE

Rayworth arrived promptly at Cedar Lane Police Station and sat in the interview room facing the detectives.

"Thanks for coming back," said Tyler. "Just a few questions we'd like to ask you. So: Stan, Ted and Roy ..."

Rayworth rolled her eyes. "Oh, I'm with you now. What a bunch! But to be fair, Stan's calmed down again; he was given a warning for being a bit rough with one or two of the girls. I never had a problem with him, personally. It was something and nothing. I'm not aware that Stacey had a problem either. *Stan Baker.* God, he's bloody ancient!"

"You know his name, then?"

"You get to know some of the regulars. Stan's rough and ready and he has this thing about slapping. But I'd say he's harmless. He doesn't try to hurt anyone; it's just a thing he's got. You have to know how to play the punters, and some of the girls they've taken on lately haven't the first clue if I'm honest. At the end of the day, we get paid for providing a service, and if all you give is attitude then you're going to end up winding some of them up. They spoke to him - Hayley, I mean, and he's cut it out so far as I know."

"And Ted Freely?"

"Same goes in my opinion. He has his 'games' as he calls them, but I'd say he's as harmless as Stan. You tell him no or you play along, the choice is yours. I don't see the problem."

"What about Roy Hately?"

"Ah, now," said Rayworth. "He's a weird one alright. And he certainly had a thing for Stacey."

"He proposed marriage to her I understand?"

"Can you believe that? Mind you, we do deal with some lonely old men, so I shouldn't be surprised." Her expression shifted into a look of dawning realisation. "You don't think ..?"

"We are exploring all possibilities at the moment," said Tyler. "Did Hately say anything to you about his feelings for Stacey?"

"He insisted on seeing her, and he asked a lot of questions about her: where she lived, who she was knocking about with, and that was more or less it. When I showed him what I've got he told me to put it away and made out he was in love."

She laughed and shook her head. "I didn't take it too personally. I got paid anyway!"

"I believe Stacey used a different name when she was working," said Tyler.

"That's right. She called herself Scarlet. She thought it sounded sexy and she didn't like the punters knowing her real name."

"Did she have a boyfriend?"

"You could say that, at a push. Dean Stewart. He was her latest. And he's a right dick. I don't know what she saw in him. I don't know how many times they broke up, or why she kept going back. But Stacey could be like that. She could blow hot and cold."

"They lived together?" asked Tyler.

"No, not as far as I know. Stacey liked her own space. She lived on her own. That's something Stewart didn't like, apparently. Bit of a control freak. But Stacey was no push over and I think that used to wind him up, not getting his own way."

39

"Was he ever violent towards her?"

"I don't know about that. She never mentioned it and I never saw any signs of it. Like I say, she was no push over, and if he'd ever laid a finger on her that would have been the end of it, I imagine. Mind you, who can say? Stacey went her own way. She was always unpredictable and you couldn't tell her anything; she would swear black was white, if she was in that kind of mood; she always had to find out for herself."

"But you didn't like Stewart?"

"I don't think he was good for Stacey. I don't think he was making her happy and I don't know why she stuck with him."

Tyler asked Rayworth if she had an address for Stewart.

"I'm not sure where he lives, but I know where he works." She gave the name of a local supermarket in Stoke, situated a mile up the road from *West End Girls.*

Mills mentioned the red headed man who had been seen watching *The Sweet Box.*

"I've seen him hanging around," said Rayworth. "He looks proper off it. You get a few like that. Maybe he's plucking up the courage, you can never tell. He's probably harmless. I suppose you've been talking to Hayley. Did she tell you about the woman who owned *The Sweet Box?*"

"There was a previous owner?" asked Mills.

"It used to be a sweet shop. An old couple ran it, and then he died, and she gives us grief sometimes. She's another one who's off it; reckons opening a brothel is disrespectful to her husband's memory."

"What kind of grief does she give you?" asked Tyler.

"She usually has a petition on the go to get us closed down. And every so often she turns up and gives us a mouthful."

"Has she made specific threats?" asked Mills.

"Not to me or the other girls personally, only to have us closed down. She hasn't managed anything yet, though, stupid cow."

Noticing the time Tyler brought the interview to a close. "You've been most helpful," he said.

"Anytime, if I can be of any help I will. I just want you to catch the sick bastard who did this."

The detectives left the station and Mills drove out beyond the city to Brown Edge, a small community nestling in the shadows of the Leek Moorlands.

Turning off the main road, they followed the narrow winding lane that ran behind Varsovia Lodge, before dipping down into the hollow, arriving finally at a large detached property where Jane and Paul Trent lived.

CHAPTER TEN

They looked a lot older than Mills had imagined. Jane Trent answered the door, and appeared to be in her late fifties. There was a distinctly stoical quality to her, he observed, so that even in grief she carried herself with a forced elegance, and spoke in a curiously measured tone that gave little away.

She ushered the two detectives through into a spacious lounge tastefully decorated and yet which bore a cold, soulless quality that the detective couldn't quite put his finger on. If this had been a show home, and Jane Trent employed to show prospective clients around, he would not have been in the least surprised.

"Paul will be down shortly," she said, her smile confined to her mouth while her eyes remained empty and lifeless. "Do take a seat," she insisted, indicating two armchairs across from a two-seater sofa separated by a small, ornate coffee table scattered with books on interior design.

"The day job?" suggested Mills, clearly hoping to display appropriate acumen.

"I beg your pardon?"

"Interior design?" said Mills.

"Oh, I see. No, I inspect schools for a living. Buying curtains and such like is a necessary indulgence."

Mills glanced over at the rather sumptuous curtains that hung down from both windows, and wondered if they were the outgoing or incoming ones. He decided not to risk commenting further on matters which he had no knowledge of or interest in and which he had always found wise to leave to a higher authority.

The detectives took their seats in the armchairs while Jane Trent remained standing. "Perhaps I can get you both a drink?" The offer seemed to come without any expectation of acceptance, and Mills politely declined and Tyler did likewise. Then the room fell into silence until somewhere upstairs the sounds of movement caused Trent to look up.

"That will be Paul now." And with that she took a seat, as though she had been relieved of her duties.

A few moments later the tall figure of Paul Trent entered the room. He held out a hand towards the detectives and shook with gusto, his gaze shifting over and through them both in turn. He had to be sixty, thought Mills, though something in his manner suggested an age well beyond that.

After greeting the visitors Trent joined his wife on the sofa.

"About ... our daughter," he said.

"Yes," said Tyler. "I'm sorry for your -"

"We don't require your sympathy," snapped Trent, "so let's get down to business, shall we." His wife looked at her husband, briefly, on the edge of reprimand, and then drew back and looked blankly in the direction of the detectives, while her husband went on. "Have you found the person responsible yet?"

Tyler started to speak, and again Trent closed him down.

"I didn't think so. But it was only a matter of time before something like this happened."

"Paul," said his wife.

"It's true, Jane, and you know it." He eyeballed Tyler. "I take it you know what *our daughter* did for a living? How she chose to ... she never wanted for anything, do you know that? Not a damned thing. If she

43

wanted something, she had it, nothing but the best. And she had brains too, oh, did she indeed. Top marks all through school, every bloody subject, and a promising start at college ... and then she met that gormless lump of shit on legs ..."

Enter Dean Stewart, thought Mills.

Trent shook his head, his hands tightening into fists.

"I understand," said Mills, "that Stacey was seeing a man named Dean Stewart."

"Was she? She might have been. We hardly saw her – hardly saw her at all anymore. It's like we ceased to exist. But I'm talking about that good for nothing moron she met at college, that Kev whatshisname ..?"

He looked to his wife for help.

"Kev Blake you mean. He played in a local band -"

"That's the one," said Trent. "High on dreams and anything he could smoke or put in a syringe. But low on talent. The damage was done by the time Stacey realised what a loser he was. She'd dropped out of college, was living in a squat in Cobridge, and feeding herself working at that place on Waterloo Road."

Trent fell silent, his hands rubbing at his face.

"Your daughter split up from Blake?" asked Tyler.

Jane Trent looked at her husband. "Last we heard from Stacey - about Kev Blake - he'd gone to Spain with another girl - gone to Ibiza, following the old hippy trail, that's what she reckoned, and good riddance all round. But Paul's right -"

"He screwed her up," said Trent, his hands pulsing into fists at his side, "he made her believe in all the crap he was feeding her, all that political nonsense, hippy stuff right out of the Marxist manifesto, and she seemed to think he was this exciting genius who was going to put the world right and make a bloody fortune no doubt while he was at it. I was all for going out there, out to wherever he's sunning himself, and kicking seven shades of shit out of him. And if I was anything like a man I would have done it, too."

"And what good would that have done?" asked his wife.

"So, who's this Dean Stewart – the latest in a long line of dropouts and layabouts, no doubt?"

Jane Trent moved forward in her seat. "Do you think that's who did this – do you think that's who killed our Stacey?"

"We have no evidence to suggest that," said Tyler. "We're still -"

"Yes, yes," said Trent, "busy going through the motions. Well, perhaps you want to come back when you've found this Stewart or whoever did it."

Tyler asked if there was anyone they knew of who might have wished to harm their daughter.

"It's like this," said Trent. "Since Stacey fell under the spell of that *Kev Blake*, she turned her back on all her old mates, and her new college friends. It was like none of them existed, same as we ceased to exist. It was as though she was ashamed of us, or something. So the people she was choosing to hang round with, we don't even know them, we don't know anything about them."

On the way out to the car Tyler said, "And before you ask, DS Mills, no, we are not booking a flight out to Ibiza to track down Kev Blake."

CHAPTER ELEVEN

Mills pulled onto the car park at Sainsbury's in Stoke town centre. It was little more than a mile from *West End Girls* and not far from Rayworth's flat.

"Now," said Tyler, "I want you to exercise some restraint."

"Sir?"

"The premises you are about to enter are known to contain a variety of food items, including many that you are known to be on good terms with."

"Thanks for the warning."

"I'm still intrigued by your current binge though. And I'm determined to get to the bottom of it."

"I wouldn't worry, sir."

"I'm not worried so much as curious."

"Well, it's simple, really ..."

Tyler looked at his watch. "Stewart is due to end his shift in five minutes. Possibly you can explain later."

"I look forward to the opportunity, sir."

The detectives made their way into the store and asked to speak to a manager. A young woman came over, looking concerned. "About the shoplifting?" she said, in a whisper.

"We believe you employ a Dean Stewart?" said Mills.

The woman brightened. "Yes, we do." *No mention of murdered girlfriends*, thought Mills. *No time off to grieve.* "He's over on the bakery. He finishes in a minute. Can I ask ..?"

"No need to bother you, really," said Tyler. "The bakery, you say?"

They made their way along the aisles, Mills attempting, theatrically, to look straight ahead as Tyler followed behind. It felt like a test, and he could feel the hunger pains beginning to announce their presence.

Even with the mandatory head covering, the ginger features of Dean Stewart were hard to miss. He was mauling trays onto a trolley, and appeared to be whistling as he worked.

"A man happy in his work," said Tyler. "Always good to see that, DS Mills."

"Looks like he hasn't a care in the world, sir."

"I wonder if we can change that."

The tray loaded, Stewart checked his watch. Four o'clock.

"Excuse me, sir," said Mills.

Five minutes later Stewart sat in the back of the unmarked car next to Tyler, with Mills in the front.

"What's this about?" asked Stewart.

"You can't make a guess?" said Mills. But Stewart looked blank. "We understand that you knew Stacey Trent."

The mists appeared to clear. "Oh, I see. That was some bad news."

"I'm taking it that you are referring to her murder?" said Mills.

"It was sick, what I heard about it. I heard it on the radio."

"You don't seem very cut up about it, if I might say so," said Mills.

"What can I say? I'm sorry and all that, but we weren't together or anything."

"I understood you were seeing her?"

"I did see her a few times, on and off, but not lately. We didn't get on."

47

"You mean that you had a falling out?" said Tyler.

"Wait a minute - you're not trying to suggest ..."

"Where were you on Sunday evening, Mr Stewart?" When a reply was not forthcoming, Tyler repeated the question.

"I was out."

"Where did you go?"

"I was out with mates, we hit a few bars."

"What time did you return home?"

"I don't know. After the pub shut I suppose."

"Midnight?"

"Something like that."

"You live local?"

"Hanley." A couple of miles up the road. "A few of us went round town, but we all had to be up for work Monday so we called it a night after last orders."

"You returned home alone?"

"Yes."

"You didn't head into Stoke, or to the West End?"

"No, why would I?"

"To meet Stacey when she finished work?"

"No. Like I said ..."

"You didn't meet her to patch things up?" suggested Mills.

"No, I didn't meet her. If she was interested she could run after me. I'd had enough of chasing after lost causes."

Tyler looked hard at Stewart. "What do you mean by that?" he said.

"Look, I'm sorry what happened to her, of course I am. But she was ..."

"Yes, Mr Stewart?"

"She was hard work. You'd arrange something and she wouldn't turn up. Or she'd work an extra shift and not tell me. And we argued about it but nothing ever changed and I had enough of it."

"You had enough of it?" said Tyler. "It sounds to me like she made you angry."

"Not like that, not like you mean."

"*Mr Stewart*?"

"Not enough to hurt her or anything - what do you take me for?"

"You didn't like the work she was doing?"

"Of course I didn't. I kept telling her to get a proper job. She wasn't stupid, she'd been to college. I said she ought to go back, train for something decent instead of catering to perverts and dirty old men for a living."

"But she wouldn't listen?" said Tyler.

"I didn't hurt her. And I didn't kill her, if that's what you're getting at."

"You mentioned that you live in Hanley."

"That's right, I do."

"Can we offer you a lift home?"

CHAPTER TWELVE

They dropped Stewart off at the Festival Flats on Town Road. Tyler watched the young man disappear inside the looming structure, and tried to work out what it was about him that didn't seem to quite add up. Then he signalled to Mills to drive on, covering the short distance to Waterloo Road.

The Sweet Box was one of a long line of terraced properties fronting the terminal drag stretching all the way into Burslem, one of the original five towns that made up Stoke on Trent. Waterloo Road was the main thoroughfare linking Burslem with the north edge of Hanley, and it constituted an infamous part of the known red light district. Streetwalkers had become synonymous with Waterloo Road, and with the many back streets that ran behind the main road.

The property was flanked by the unoccupied *Furniture Mine* on one side, and a newsagent on the other. The front door was closed, and a small sign in the front window proclaimed that the business was closed for the day but would be open as usual on the following day.

Mills parked up fifty yards away on the opposite side, close to two other cars. It was a little after five.

"Bit early," he said.

"The early bird is supposed to catch the worms," said Tyler.

"I can eat most things," said Mills, "but even I have limits. They would have to be pickled. What do you make of Dean Stewart?"

"On the face of it, he sounds plausible enough," said Tyler. "He has no alibi for Sunday night. But that might count in his favour. If he'd planned anything, I'd imagine he'd factor in some kind of an alibi, he seems too switched on not to. On the other hand, if it was an innocent meeting with Stacey Trent that turned violent ..."

Tyler thought for a minute. "He wasn't there to meet her when her shift finished, or else Rayworth would presumably have mentioned it. He could have met up with her along the way, but then he wouldn't have known that she was planning to walk home."

"He could have been waiting around the corner," said Mills, "and then followed her."

"He could have done. But that suggests sinister intent, and therefore the need for an alibi. And the location of her flat in relation to where she was found ... it wouldn't make sense to cut through the lido."

"It was a nice evening for a walk, sir," offered Mills.

"I don't doubt it. But it was midnight when her shift ended. I don't buy that she was just taking in the air, though I could be wrong."

"You think she was meeting someone?"

"That seems more likely. It's a discreet location; at least it is at that time on a Sunday night, as far as I'm aware."

"I'd agree," said Mills.

"But if she was meeting someone ..."

"It's likely they would be the last person to see her alive."

"But was that person Dean Stewart?"

A man was walking towards them on the opposite side of the road. From the distance of a few hundred yards he appeared to match the description of the man who had been watching *The Sweet Box*.

"I'd say that's ginger hair hiding under that cap," said Tyler.

"You could be right, sir. There seems to be a lot of it about suddenly."

Tyler glanced at him. "This isn't a Sherlock Holmes adventure, remember that."

"I'll try to, sir."

The man was almost at *The Sweet Box*. The detectives watched carefully, but the man's gaze seemed fixed ahead, and he didn't appear to even notice the closed door, or the sign in the window, continuing instead on his way down the road towards Hanley.

"Should we mark him down as a no show?" said Mills.

"Stomach beginning to rumble, is it? You never did explain the workings of your most mysterious new diet." Tyler checked the time. "Our man has an hour yet at least; ample time for you to solve at least one of the mysteries running around my head."

Mills sighed. "You're going to be disappointed, sir."

"In you or your story?"

"It's barely even a story. The fact is, she's booked me in for a well man check. I've been rumbled."

"Curiouser and curiouser," said Tyler. "Am I missing something here? You imagine, do you, that they offer prizes at the well man clinic for the most impressive weight gain?"

"I wish," said Mills. "No, I'm afraid, despite her distractions, she's noticed I've been putting the pounds back on, and I'm booked in next week with the nurse."

Tyler shook his head. "No, I'm still not getting it. Perhaps you ought to be writing mystery stories in your spare time."

"I know it doesn't make sense. But think of it like this, sir: the condemned man's last meal."

"Ah, the clouds are clearing away now, the weights falling from my eyes. You are stuffing yourself to the gills before the canteen finally closes down."

"Something like that, sir."

"The condemned man's final few dozen meals."

"I'm not proud of myself."

"Suspect returning," said Tyler.

"What's that?"

Tyler was looking in the wing mirror. "Our man, having crossed the road, now appears to be approaching us from behind."

They watched the man go past, looking to see if he was taking any interest in *The Sweet Box* across the road.

He continued on his way, striding purposefully back up the road without even a glance in the direction of the property in question.

"Looks like a false alarm," said Mills.

"Possibly. Look, park up in the side street behind us." Tyler got out of the car. "I'll radio you if I need to."

As Mills swung the car around and headed into the indicated street, Tyler walked into one of the shop doorways, one with the door set well back, and watched as the man disappeared in the distance. It was heading towards six when he clocked the same man heading back down Waterloo Road, striding out once again, this time on the opposite side of the road from *The Sweet Box*. Tyler was on the same side, a good sixty yards beyond where *The Sweet Box* was situated. The road was almost deserted of people, with a scattering of traffic still moving in both directions.

The man was almost level with *The Sweet Box*, Tyler stepping back into the recess, expecting him to come rattling past.

The seconds ticked by, and the DCI peered out of the recess to see the man standing directly opposite *The Sweet Box*.

He wasn't moving; standing statue-still, hands at his sides, and staring in the direction of the property. Then he moved quickly, without warning, making his way across the road, scrutinising the sign in the window. After a few moments he stepped back and turned to move away, only to find Tyler blocking his path.

"Excuse me, sir."

The man bolted, back in the direction of Burslem, Tyler taking off after him. He was moving at pace, but Tyler had been clocking up the miles for years, and he was closing in. They were almost at the traffic lights at the top of the road, no more than a few yards between them and the brow of the hill, when the man stopped and turned around, fists clenched, his face set in a menacing snarl.

"What do you want?"

Tyler took out his ID and flashed it. "I want a word."

The man took off again, but Tyler was on him, turning him around by the shoulder. A fist lashed out, and the detective instinctively ducked, the blow only grazing the side of his head as it found thin air; and then Tyler had him down on the ground, pinning him to the pavement next to a dried-out patch of vomit, radioing Mills to bring the car round.

CHAPTER THIRTEEN

"No comment."

The only words the man had uttered in close on forty minutes.

The duty solicitor had confirmed the man's name as Eric Faron, his address Flat 38 Queen Anne Flats, Burslem. And now he made a third contribution.

"I'm not aware that Mr Faron has broken any laws. He has simply stood outside a property on Waterloo Road, read a sign on display in the window, and after being harassed and chased along the public highway, and naturally in a state of panic as a consequence, he attempted to defend himself because he believed, understandably, that he was being attacked."

Tyler turned back to Faron. "Where were you on Sunday evening?"

"No comment."

"A young woman, working at *The Sweet Box*, the property that you have been watching for weeks now, Mr Faron, was attacked and killed on Sunday evening. And I want to know where you were when this attack took place."

"No comment."

"If you can supply an alibi for the time in question, Mr Faron -"

"No comment."

"Mr Faron," said the duty solicitor, "has no criminal record. He has no history of attacking prostitutes, or anyone else, for that matter."

"Not as yet," said Tyler.

"Meaning?"

"A charge of assaulting a police officer in the course of his duties is pending."

"Are you being serious?"

"Why wouldn't I be?" said Tyler. "Mr Faron was acting suspiciously, and in the course of my attempting to speak to him about his actions, he fled and then proceeded to throw a punch at me, causing me to make an arrest in accordance with procedure. And if his behaviour did not arouse suspicions in me, then I would hardly be doing my job. I am investigating a murder, and the victim worked on the premises that Mr Faron -"

"You've said all of that once already."

"And now I'm saying it again." Tyler's tone was rising, and Mills felt the old familiar crackle of tension filling the room. "I'm repeating myself for the benefit of Mr Faron. I want him to be in no doubt that his continued attempts to be unhelpful -"

"Mr Faron has the right to remain silent -"

"Can only deepen suspicions that he has something to hide -"

"Either charge Mr Faron or else let him go."

Tyler stopped talking. Mills waited, not moving a muscle. The stillness in the room felt like the moments before the bomb explodes.

"As you wish," said Tyler. "Mr Faron, you are free to go."

Mills followed the DCI up the stairs to the CID office. "Did I miss something?" he asked as they reached the top.

"I want Faron followed," said Tyler. "I want him watched around the clock."

"But won't this look like ..?"

"What?"

"Well, like a grudge or something, against Faron?"

"I don't care what it looks like. I want him under surveillance starting immediately. I want to know what he does all day, apart from standing outside local brothels."

Tyler picked up his coat. "I'll be back in an hour."

*

Tyler knocked on the door of *West End Girls* until Hayley Greener appeared.

"Can't you read – we're closed!" She squinted out at the DCI. "Oh, it's you. Have you found out something?"

"Can I come in?"

She led him along the now familiar corridor through to her office at the rear of the building.

"How well did you know Stacey Trent?" he asked once they were both seated.

"I knew her professionally, but not socially. That's true of all my staff. She was popular with the punters."

"Did she ever talk to you about her personal life?"

"You mean boyfriends, stuff like that?" She shook her head. "Not really. I get to know some of the girls, but Stacey kept herself to herself. I know she knocked about with Christine a bit. But they were chalk and cheese those two."

"How do you mean?"

"I keep my ears open, of course; you have to in this line of work, and you pick up bits here and there. I know Christine had a rough time of it growing up. I understand that she was in care, and didn't really know her parents. It's not an unusual story in this game I'm afraid to say. You don't get many born with the silver spoon drifting in here, not in my experience."

She stood up and switched on the kettle that stood above a small fridge. "Cuppa?"

57

While the kettle boiled Greener, sitting back down, went on. "That's why Stacey was different, I would say. She came from a different place entirely. Like I said, I don't know a lot about her, but I heard she had well to do folks, and it does make you wonder, naturally."

Greener made two coffees and handed one to Tyler.

"And what does all that wondering amount to?" he asked, before sipping his drink.

"Not a lot. But I do have a reputation for being something of a 'nosy bitch' as some of my girls will verify. I was curious about Stacey, and I wondered why she was doing this for a living when it seemed like she had other options. I've been around the block, and more than a few times, so I've seen lot of different types come and go. Some you just can't fathom."

"Was Stacey Trent one of those?"

"I suppose she was. She seemed to like the work, and maybe the seediness of it appealed to her; it's hard to put into words. For most it was a job, a dirty job to make ends meet, to pay the rent, feed a habit. But Stacey ... she appeared to relish the work for its own sake, as far as I could tell."

"And apart from the punters you've already named, you're not aware of anyone else, at either place, who ..?"

Greener shook her head. "There was no-one else I can think of, no-one who stands out."

"Does the name Eric Faron mean anything to you?"

"Should it?" She thought for a few moments and took a drink of her coffee. "I can't say that it does." Then her eyes narrowed and she grinned. "He's the guy who's been watching *The Sweet Box*?"

Tyler retained a neutral expression and took another sip of his drink.

"You think it's him?"

"I'm not saying that."

"He's a weird enough creep, no question of that. He's unsettled a few of the girls lately, just his presence. I suppose it's only a matter of time before someone like that starts acting up."

Tyler took another drink. She was fishing; he let her continue.

"Stands to reason that when someone starts hanging around like that, and with a look about him, too ... something's going on, as sure as eggs are eggs. Unless he's employed by someone to put everyone on edge, you know: *intimidation*."

An idea occurred to her, or else an old idea, already fully formed, and which she now chose to air. "Maybe he's employed by Hackett."

"Hackett?"

"The previous owner." Greener took another drink and looked at Tyler. "Before I took it over it was a sweet shop. *The Sweet Box*."

"You kept the name."

"Why not – it seemed to work. Husband and wife used to run it as a sweet shop, had been running it for years, and then he drops dead of a stroke, or his heart, something like that. Anyway, she kept the shop going for a short time and then decided to sell up, and that's when I moved in."

"When was this?"

"A year and a half, something like that. It was a few months after that when she stopped me in the street one day, out of the blue, came up to me and had a right go, about how it was a scandal me running a place like that and soiling her husband's memory. That's the word she actually used: '*soiled*'.

"Then I got a letter, a few weeks later, pushed through the door, saying the same things and telling me that if I had any decency or shame I would close the place down and have some respect for the dead.

"And it's kept on ever since. I get letters from time to time threatening that she'll take me to court."

"Any other threats?"

"Nothing sinister, if that's what you mean. In one of the letters she said I should at least take the original sign down. That it was in bad taste."

"And what did you think about that?" asked Tyler.

"To be honest, when I thought about it ... I thought, perhaps she has a point. I'm a reasonable person; I'm not in the business of winding people up."

Greener took another drink and looked again at Tyler. "It was just after that, and I was seriously considering taking the sign down, replacing it, when she stopped me in the street again as I was getting in my car. She had another go, shouting and bawling she was, telling me that I would burn in hell for my sins."

Greener finished her drink. "Well, as you can probably imagine, her attitude got the better of me, and all thoughts of taking the sign down ... well, I thought, stuff her, talking to me like that. I'll be damned if I'll take it down now."

Tyler placed his cup down and nodded. "So, you wonder if she's employing a different tactic: getting someone to stand outside your premises, intimidating the staff so that they stop working for you."

"You hear of stranger things, don't you? Nothing much would surprise me anymore."

CHAPTER FOURTEEN

When Tyler returned to Cedar Lane Police Station he noted a change in atmosphere the instant he walked through the door. A new kind of tension; something was cracking off.

He walked up to the CID office to find DS Mills at his desk working away on a report, a half eaten chocolate digestive clutched resolutely in his left hand.

"Multi-tasking I see," said Tyler.

Mills looked up from his report and demolished the biscuit, as though further hesitation may have resulted in confiscation. "Carstairs has arrived," he said. "He asked about you."

"How thoughtful of him. Your initial impressions?"

"I'm hanging fire, sir."

"Wise man. Have we got an officer on Faron yet?"

"We have, but I don't think it'll hold. I understand Carstairs is already aware of it and making noises."

"We'll see, then."

"Been anywhere nice?"

He told Mills about his visit back to *West End Girls*, and his conversation with Hayley Greener.

"Interesting, but it has to be coincidental," said Mills. "I mean, intimidation is one thing, if that's what it is. But murder's a bit strong."

Tyler laughed. "Murder's always a 'bit strong' wouldn't you say? But I agree, on the face of it. Having said that, we don't know who we're dealing with, do we? I had the impression that Greener might wish to play me."

"Play you, sir?"

"Take that schoolboy look off your face, DS Mills."

"Right away, sir."

"I suspect she saw an opportunity to get this Hackett woman off her back. Whether there's more to it, though ... she could be off her head, crazed by grief and this perceived insult to the memory of her husband; and Faron could be a raging psycho on the edge, the two of them in cahoots maybe. But need I go on with this banal speculation?"

"I get the point, sir."

"Then my work is done."

Tyler's phone was ringing. It was an internal call.

Mills glanced over. "Looks like the new Chief's eager to meet you," he said.

*

Tyler had made the visit to CS Berkins' office countless times; and whilst Berkins had proven himself to be an exception to the rule, in Tyler's experience - a figure of authority who used his position of power to try to do some good in the world; to effect change in a positive way, and to support those beneath him in the chain of command ... despite all of that, Tyler had always made that short trip with a sense of foreboding. The shadows of the past were never, it seemed, more prone to making their dark presence felt, than when he found himself *summoned*.

Carstairs appeared to glare at him by way of welcome, and pointed to the seat opposite. "DCI Tyler, I don't believe that we have met."

"If we have done, then I don't recall it."

Even as the words came out, Tyler recognised the sharpness, the edge of vitriol that he simply could not contain in a situation like this. The words were out there now, beyond recall, and he watched Carstairs carefully, his every nerve and sinew seemingly alive and on high alert. Was that a slight raising of the eyebrows, an acknowledgement of the first warning shots across the bows?

Carstairs asked about the current case, and Tyler brought the senior man up to speed.

"No clues from forensics?"

If there were, don't you think I might be acting on them?

"We know that the likely weapon was a Stanley knife. The fatal wound to the throat, along with the facial slashing, done with a razor blade, and the pressure applied suggests a handled device. So, some kind of carpet cutting tool would seem likely."

Tyler was spelling it out like he was talking to a first year student. He could almost taste the insubordination rising in his throat, and couldn't seem to quell it.

"There doesn't appear to have been much of a struggle. There is no material found under the victim's fingernails consistent with a fight, and the suggestion is that the woman was surprised. The fatal wound administered quickly, the mutilation following afterwards. The mutilation might suggest anger, even hatred, implying that this was in some way personal; or else simply a sadistic act carried out by a stranger. At this stage we don't know."

"I understand that you have authorised surveillance on Eric Faron?"

"That is correct."

"Can you explain why you didn't seek the necessary authorisation for that?"

"I needed to act quickly, and we were in between chief superintendents at the time."

Carstairs' eyes narrowed, the face, all cheek bones and nose, thin lips and twitching ears, constricting further into a spiteful countenance that Tyler had seen dozens of times and usually in men sitting behind imposing desks.

"You have something of a reputation for striking out on your own terms, DCI Tyler, and I'm afraid that I don't have the time to waste on checking up on senior officers and in issuing reprimands. Mavericks have no place, these days, that's common enough knowledge, and I will not tolerate them on my watch. How Chief Superintendent Berkins chose to operate is not my particular concern, but I warn you: I am not he. Understood?"

"I understand that you are not Graham Berkins," said Tyler, his expression unwavering.

"You will pull off the surveillance on Faron with immediate effect, and if you feel that it ought to be re-instated, then you will go through the correct channels and argue your case effectively, is that clear?"

"Very clear," said Tyler.

The first meeting was over, and the detective made his way back through to the office, where he found Mills sitting at his desk nervously munching on a fresh chocolate biscuit.

"How did it go?" he asked.

Tyler smiled. "Danny Mills – I do believe that you were worried about me."

"Well, I did wonder."

"You really shouldn't fret. We have one good man down on account of an ulcerated gut already."

Mills appeared to relax, but the effect was marginal. "Did he – did Carstairs – have much to say?"

"He said enough. But let me put your mind at rest: he and I are going to get along like a house on fire."

CHAPTER FIFTEEN

Mills drove along Leek Road, turning at the crossroads beyond the crematorium, towards the village of Milton. "Carstairs has pulled the plug on us watching Faron," he said. "What do you think about that?"

"I'm hardly surprised," said Tyler.

"You had your doubts it would yield anything?"

"I meant, new brooms always feel inclined to find a floor to sweep, whether it needs sweeping or not."

"You think Carstairs will bring in changes?"

"I'd be amazed if he didn't. But the hope is that Berkins won't be away too long, so our new broom is hardly likely to implement total revolution. He'll still have to make his mark, though. Careers of his kind depend on such things; they can't be seen to leave well alone on any account. It's an unwritten rule."

Mills parked up in a quiet street beyond the village centre.

"I imagine Greener will keep us informed as to whether our encounter with Faron has dented his enthusiasm for standing outside *The Sweet Box*. We'll see." Tyler got out of the car. "And so our attentions turn to Val Hackett. She sounded quite reasonable over the phone. I actually got the impression that she relished the prospect of our visit. Another opportunity to plead her case I suspect. Get *The Sweet Box* closed down."

The house was a modest terraced property, but it had clearly been lovingly maintained, with latticed sash windows and a varnished black front door polished to give a certain front door in Downing Street a run for its money.

Mrs Hackett opened the gleaming door and welcomed in her visitors with a beaming smile. Her diminutive frame led the way through to a snug lounge area, velvet drapes hanging down to frame both windows. "Do please make yourselves comfortable," she said, gesturing the detectives towards a small sofa. "Tea?"

There was something assured in her tone, suggesting that to decline the offer of a drink was not an option. She quickly returned with a tray of refreshments, which she set down on a small table between the detectives and her own small armchair. Mills observed her to be in her mid to late sixties, in good health, and with a ruddy complexion that appeared to breathe fire.

After she had poured out the tea, she invited her guests to help themselves to milk and sugar. An assortment of biscuits filled up the rest of the table, and Mills licked his lips instinctively but resolved to fight temptation valiantly.

"How good of you to call," she said, once additives to the drinks had been satisfactorily administered.

"I'm afraid this is hardly a social call," said Tyler, though the host's beaming smile was not dented in the slightest by his remark.

"I appreciate that you must be very busy. It's the world we live in, I'm sorry to say. I understand that you would like to discuss *The Sweet Box*."

Mills caught Tyler's eye and stifled a smile. But before Tyler could respond to the question, Hackett cut in: "Phil used to love that business, running the sweet shop, I mean. I did too, I won't lie about it.

"We ran it for the best part of forty years, do you know that? I wonder where all the time went, sometimes I do; seems to have flashed by. I question if we'd have been running it still, if it wasn't for Phil's stroke. Tried to keep the business going, I did, but it was too much for me, and it wasn't the same without dear old Phil. We were a team, you know. We were famous, in our own little way. I miss it. I miss him."

She took a drink and as she did so her eyes seemed to retain their focus on old memories.

"I understand that you were ... somewhat disappointed," said Tyler, "when you found out the nature of the business that took over -"

She snapped out of her reverie. "*Disappointed*? I suppose that's one word you could use, if you were desperate enough. If the choice on offer was limited; but I'd go a lot stronger than that myself: I was *outraged*, I tell you straight, and if I was given to using swear words, which I'm not and never have been – and neither was my old Phil, for that matter – well, I'd turn this room blue in an instant! Disgusting, that's the word I'd use. And I was disgusted!"

"Mrs Hackett," started Tyler.

"We sold any sweet you could name; we had the lot we did. Jars and jars of them, and the fancy stuff as well, boxes of toffees and chocolates that would make you dribble down your shirts just to look at them; we had something for any occasion you could think of, and the kids used to love coming in, the after school lot – and some of them before school too, the little monkeys!"

Her face was fairly glowing with the memories as she stepped into her stride. The detectives each took a sip of their drinks and tacitly agreed to let her run free for a few minutes longer.

The woman waxed lyrical about a golden age of sugary treats, and the public service that she and Phil had offered that corner of the Potteries for more than a quarter of a century.

"... because it wasn't just a business, you know – okay, so at the end of the day we had bills to pay like anyone else; but it was more than that: we were serving our community, we were, me and my lovely, lovely man, bless his memory."

Tyler coughed, catching her attention.

"And we'd have had a range of cough sweets for that, too, everything from Fisherman's Friends to Jakeman's to -"

"I believe that you've been involved in a campaign to have the present business closed down," said Tyler.

"I've organised petitions, spoke to my MP, written to the Prime Minister – fat lot of good any of that does you. They don't want to know, those who don't have to live with it on their doorstep. Okay, so it isn't exactly on my doorstep, living here, but if it was any other business that had taken over, I would have been proud to call in and tell them how it used to be, with me and Phil, if they didn't already know – but the type who run those kinds of places, they don't want to know about what decent people do. They're scum, that's what they are – scum!"

The anger came quickly, and was startling in its vehemence; and then it was gone just as quickly, replaced once again with a charming, sweet smile.

"More tea?"

Before the detectives left, they asked about Eric Faron.

"I don't recall that name. Who is he?"

As Hackett showed them out she pointed to the framed photograph of her husband on the wall in the hallway.

"Ten years ago, that was taken. That's him, that's my Phil, there, behind the counter. And that's how I remember him best. They were good times, they were, and no mistake. They were the best times. But they're gone now. Still, never mind. If I can get that filthy place shut down Phil can rest easy in his grave, and I can follow on behind him when the Good Lord thinks I'm ready."

CHAPTER SIXTEEN

Mills blew out his cheeks as he drove back to base.

"Go on, then, say it," said Tyler.

"I don't know if I can bring myself to, sir. I know she's grieving and all that, but, really, could a sweet little lady like her ... no; I just can't make the leap. I just can't see Mrs Hackett carving someone up."

"And that's your last word, is it? No alibi, a clear motive, but on the grounds that she reminds you of your grandmother, she couldn't possibly stoop to murder?"

"You haven't seen my grandmother," said Mills. "Big, tough, harsh woman, rippling muscles, calloused hands and a tone that could cut an iron bar – now she definitely would stoop to murder!"

"She sounds like a figure in a fairy tale."

"Well, she'd have baked you in an oven if she caught you wandering the woods after dark."

"Finished?" said Tyler.

"Finished, sir. Back in the drawer for another time, bless her."

"Then let's head into Stoke."

"Any particular reason?"

"I believe we're looking for Corporation Street, are you familiar with it?"

"I think I can find it."

A few minutes later the car rolled up outside a small block of flats. "Number sixteen," said Tyler looking across at the tired building as he got out of the car.

"Rayworth?" asked Mills.

"Bear with me."

The flat was on the first floor, a few doors from the stairwell, and Tyler knocked on. Failing to get a response he waited, listening, before trying again.

"I take it we're calling on spec?" said Mills.

The door opened, and a dishevelled young man looked out. "Yes?"

"I'm looking for Christine Rayworth," said Tyler.

"Who are you?"

Tyler flashed his ID badge.

"To do with the murder, is it?"

"Is Miss Rayworth in?"

"Chris!" the young man shouted. "Cops – for you." He retreated back inside the flat, leaving the door open behind him. The detectives followed him inside.

The main living area was almost entirely bare, two large beanbags and a small TV. The young man disappeared into a room beyond, and almost immediately Rayworth emerged from the same room, wearing a dirty off-white dressing gown that reached down to just above her knees, revealing bare legs.

"Have you found something?" she said. "I wasn't expecting you."

"Just a few questions," said Tyler.

"Fire away," she said, and then glanced behind her in the direction of the other room. "It's alright if Jon's here?" she said. "I mean, it's nothing confidential?"

"He's welcome to join us," said Tyler.

"He wouldn't know anything."

"Your boyfriend?"

"Excuse for one. No, I'm joking, he's alright. Been having a run of bad luck lately, lost his job on the market. He's looking for something better now."

"Sorry to hear he lost his job," said Tyler.

72

"Accused him of thieving, cheeky bast – sorry, I mean -"

"No, please, do go on."

"Not a lot to it, really: they said he had his hand in the till, Jon said he didn't, they couldn't prove anything and he told them to stuff it. Said if he couldn't be trusted then they could stick it where the sun doesn't shine. You can't blame him, can you? So, anyway, what questions have you got?"

Tyler looked towards the other room, and then back at Rayworth.

"Don't worry about him," she said, "he's gone back to bed. Needs his twelve hours a day or he's fit for nothing. You'll hear him snoring any minute."

"I'd like you to call in at the station," said Tyler.

"I can answer your questions here."

But something in the eye of the DCI caused her to acquiesce. "Give me two minutes," she said.

*

Rayworth was shown to an interview room and provided with a drink. Outside, Mills looked at Tyler. "Are you going to give me a clue?"

"I haven't much of one myself. I'm running on instinct, pure and simple. I wanted to see Rayworth in her home environment."

"And?"

"She was keen to bad-mouth Stacey Trent's boyfriend, Dean Stewart. Maybe her own boyfriend has qualities not yet apparent."

"I don't follow," said Mills.

"That's possibly because I'm not making a lot of sense. Something isn't adding up, that's all, and I'm trying to make it add up and get to the bottom of it. And when I get there, there might be nothing to find. Let's see, shall we."

They made their way into the interview room and took their seats opposite Rayworth.

"Thanks again for coming in," said Tyler.

"No probs. You do a decent coffee, I'll give you that," she said.

"Really?" Tyler looked across at Mills. "Did you hear that? We'll have all sorts drifting in if word gets out."

"So what do you want to know?"

"You mentioned, the last time we spoke, about Stacey's boyfriend: Dean Stewart. You didn't sound keen, if I remember correctly."

She shrugged. "He's nothing to me."

"You didn't seem to think he was good for Stacey."

"Not my idea of fun, but it was up to her who she knocked about with."

"But they were together, as far as you knew?"

"I thought so, yes."

"Based on what?"

"Look – is there a problem?"

"Was she seeing anyone else?"

"If she was, I wasn't aware of it."

She looked at Tyler, and then across at Mills, and finally back to Tyler. "Is Stewart saying he wasn't with her?"

Tyler paused for a moment, and then he said: "Do you know anything about the history of *The Sweet Box* – before it became what it is now?"

Rayworth frowned. "How do you mean?"

"Are you aware that it was formerly a sweet shop?"

"Oh, I see. I know that mad bitch who used to run it has been making trouble."

"What kind of trouble?"

"I heard there were petitions to have the place closed down. We had a few police raids, anonymous calls saying there were illegal activities going on. Hayley said she thought it would have been that bitch doing it most likely."

"She never confronted you, or any of the other women working there?"

"She did, once or twice, but not recently. She stood outside yelling her head off that it was obscene or something like that. That it was disrespectful to her dead husband. You get nutters, though, don't you? I don't think it bothered any of the girls; she was hardly frightening. I'd say she was sad more than anything."

"You work a rota, I believe?" said Tyler. "Regular hours?"

"More or less. Sometimes we cover as well, and you get slack times and busy periods, like most businesses, I suppose."

"Do you have regular days off?"

Rayworth looked puzzled by the DCI's questioning. "I don't mind much what days I work. It's all the same to me. I do seven days a week sometimes, most times if I can. I have bills to pay. Rent isn't cheap, not even in Stoke."

"Did Stacey need the hours?"

"What are you getting at?"

"I'm trying to build up a picture. Did she need the money?"

"She had rent to pay, same as me. Oh, I get it - you mean because she had family? That's true enough, but I don't think she had much to do with them. So yes, she needed the work."

"Seven days a week?"

"Not quite. She always had Monday evenings off."

"For any particular reason?"

"If there was, she never said."

"Okay," said Tyler. "Thank you."

"That's it?"

"Unless you can think of anything else that might be of interest." He looked at Mills. "Do you have anything you'd like to ask?"

"Not at the present time," said Mills, and his tone was as stiff as his expression.

"Then we'll leave it there for now," said Tyler. "I expect you'll want to get back to your boyfriend."

"No hurry on that score," she said.

"I hope he finds a new job soon. Then he can pull his weight with the rent."

She laughed at that. "He lives with his folks. There will always be a roof over *his* head. Some of us aren't so lucky."

"You don't have family in the city?"

"I don't have family. I was in care. My mother was a heroin addict, dead a long time; I never knew who my father was and I don't much care to know. Some people have all the luck, don't they?"

"Some people?" asked Tyler.

"You know how it goes."

"Are you talking about Stacey?"

"Well, she did have a choice, at the end of the day. She could have gone back begging to mummy and daddy. I heard they were loaded. It's a bit like that song, you know, the one about *common people*; about the rich, or some of them, thinking they know what it's like to be poor by slumming it for a while."

"And you think that fits Stacey?"

"I don't know. We were kind of mates, but we came from different places, and I don't know if you can ever get around that entirely."

"What do you mean?"

"Oh, I don't know what I'm talking about. Maybe I'm just bitter and twisted because I didn't have the chances some people have. Or I'm just feeling sorry for myself and need to snap out of it. I could do something else; make a proper go of something. But some days – most days, if I'm honest – you just think, what's the point? You think: this is who I am, what I've got, so make the most of it."

They showed Rayworth out and made their way back up to the office.

"I don't know what I would have done without you there, DS Mills."

Mills sat at his desk and reached for the biscuits, setting off into them at pace. Tyler watched him in an attitude of fascination, until Mills halted mid munch.

"What?"

"Come on, then," said Tyler, "get it off your chest."

"Nothing to get off my chest, sir."

"I've known you long enough, Danny. So, come on: out with it."

Mills placed the biscuits, what was left of the packet, down on the desk.

"Since you ask ..."

"Yes?"

"Some sort of a briefing might have been helpful. At least then I might have a blind clue where we're heading."

Tyler acknowledged the point with a nod of his head. "I see. And if I had a blind clue, I would have shared it with you, gladly."

Mills didn't appear convinced.

"The sad fact is that I'm stuck on this one, Danny, I really am. But some voice deep down inside keeps repeating names like Rayworth and Stewart and I can't quite see why, not yet."

"You think it could be her?" said Mills, reaching once again for the biscuits, stopping himself in the nick of time. "You think she killed Stacey Trent? Why – because Trent was born with the silver spoon and Rayworth was born on the wrong side of a needle?"

"You have quite a poetic turn of phrase when you put your mind to it, did anyone ever tell you that?"

"My English teacher once called me a waste of space."

"Teachers, in my experience, are rarely good talent spotters. And no, I don't think it's quite as simple as that, and I'm not even saying that I think Rayworth was responsible. Just that she might hold the key, that's all."

"And Stewart?"

"Same goes."

"I still don't follow," said Mills. "I know I'm just a brain dead native of these parts -"

"I've never thought that for a second, and you know it."

"Jim -"

"Look, I'll spell it out, what little of it there is to spell out. Because it's all to do with feelings, gut feelings that I can't quite seem to articulate. When Rayworth first told us about Stewart I had the feeling that she was feeding us. That she was painting a portrait of a dead loss boyfriend who might fit the frame. And naturally, with my suspicious nature, that made me wonder about her, what she was up to."

"And ..?"

"Now I'm less sure about my suspicions."

"So what's changed?"

Tyler held Mills' gaze and a knowing look entered his eye. "Give me some credit, Danny."

"Credit for what?"

"You think we have something in common, me and Rayworth, growing up on the wrong side of the tracks - you think that makes me look at her differently? That suddenly – what, she's now the salt of the earth?"

"I didn't say any of that."

"You didn't need to. It's there, under the surface though isn't it?"

"Jim," said Mills, "for God's sake. I think more of you than that."

At the sound of his name, Tyler appeared to crumple from within.

"Do you want to talk about it?" said Mills, offering what was left of the biscuits.

CHAPTER SEVENTEEN

The children had gone to bed and Mills sat in front of the TV as the medical drama played out to its long-anticipated conclusion.

"A drink, Danny?" his wife asked him as the credits came up.

Low cal hot chocolate was back on the menu, though not a word had been spoken about calorie intake for weeks, and Mills could hardly stand the suspense. She handed him his drink and sat down next to him. For the second time that day he was invited to get it off his chest.

"Okay, I won't deny it; I've been backsliding a bit. I'm sick of eating this and not eating that. I watched Stoke play last weekend and I had three pies and as many pints. In the canteen at work I've been hitting the bacon and cheese, twice some days, and I'm not even going to tell you about the sausage rolls and the cake stand at the -"

"Danny."

"Yes?"

"I love you."

His eyes clouded with suspicion. Was this some devilish tactic in the game?

"I'm worried about your health because I love you. But I don't want to see you unhappy."

He placed a guilty hand across his gut. "I've got the fatness back ... if it ever went away. It's not a nice thing to look at, I know that."

"I love you as you are, Danny. And anyway, I don't go in for the skinny types. But I want you around for many years to come, and so do your children." She kissed him. "I booked you in for a well man check because I hate the thought of anything happening to you."

Her eyes filled up and Mills pulled her towards him, their cups of low cal chocolate meeting with a loud crash, the contents soaking both of them.

*

A little while later, they were both sitting up in bed, red faced with exertion. "Well, that's a load off my mind," he said, and she slapped his arm. "And fair point, I shouldn't be so out of breath."

"It isn't flattering, you're right." Then she laughed.

"What is it?"

"The funny thing is, when I asked you to get it off your chest, I thought you were going to tell me about work."

He told her about developments in the case, or the lack of them, and of Tyler's outburst of emotion when Mills had plucked up courage and asked him about the Scene of Crime officer he had been seeing, and who had since been posted down to London.

"So, it's off, it's over?"

"Looks like it."

"But – London's no distance?"

"He won't set foot in the place."

"Not even for love?"

"Not for anything."

"But - she could visit him back here?"

"I think they fell out about it, or at least Jim did. He falls out easily."

"He didn't want her to accept the promotion?"

"No, he urged her to go for it."

"You mean, to get rid of her?"

"It didn't sound that way. I think he wanted what's best for her, and felt he was likely to be a liability. I don't think he could believe his luck when they got together, and he never believed that good fortune could hold. He's back where he started."

"That's sad. And this new boss?"

"It couldn't have happened at a worse time. Carstairs is the sort who'll bring out the demons in him."

Then he told her about the latest interview with Rayworth. "I was out of order, I shouldn't have said anything. In fact I hardly did say anything. But I suppose it was implied when I asked him what had changed – I mean, with Rayworth mentioning her past, being in care and all that."

"But you still have to do your job, Danny. You can't keep walking on eggshells."

"Jim's touchy about his past. And I shouldn't have questioned his professional judgement. We don't know where we're going with this case, Carstairs is on our backs and set to get worse, and Jim's like a powder keg. All in all, you could say what a great time for a diet!" His wife was looking hard at him. "Did I say 'diet' when of course I mean 'lifestyle change'?"

The bedroom fell silent.

"She must have been meeting someone," he said. "It was getting late, she lived only yards from where she was killed; but it isn't a short cut to her flat. She would have to have purposefully over shot."

"It was a nice evening. Maybe she just wasn't ready to go home. If she was meeting someone, she could have met them at her flat. Do you think someone followed her when she left work?"

"Someone meeting her, someone following her, it's all possible."

At some point the speculations petered out and Mills and his wife settled down to sleep. Mills caught it quickly, and was soon dreaming that he was queuing up for pies at the game on Saturday. There were five pies left in the display cabinet, and he was sixth in the queue. And then there were four pies, three ... two. The last pie waited alone, one customer ahead of him. The customer in front was a small woman and quite old. She didn't look like a pie-eater; but she was hesitating, looking from the solitary pie to the new stand of health bars, unable to decide.

His stomach was crying, she was pointing at the bars, he could have kissed her. And then she pointed decisively at the last pie, and Mills screamed.

CHAPTER EIGHTEEN

Mills was already at his desk when Tyler arrived.

"You couldn't sleep either?"

"Funny you should mention that, sir."

"Oh?"

"I think I've got a problem."

Tyler sat down. "You know what they say about a problem shared."

That's rich, thought Mills, coming from the world's worst sharer of problems, and a man who instead of talking insisted on going for insane runs through the city to let out some of that pent up energy.

Not given to physical exertion beyond the bedroom, and not having gone out for a run since his schooldays, Mills shared the load, telling Tyler about his anxiety dream.

"So, you're saying you have a problem with pies?"

"I'm saying I have a problem with food. I was screaming, she had to wake me up, and all because I was afraid that the woman ahead of me in the queue at the match was going to take the last pie. And then, when I finally got back off to sleep, the crowd – the entire bloody crowd, home supporters and away supporters, all of them were singing:

"Who ate all the pies?

"He did, he did – Mills ate all the pies!"

"And so the diet begins again in earnest?"

"I have to call it a lifestyle change. But yes, you're going to see a new version of DS Mills. It's not going to be an easy time."

"Thanks for the warning."

"You say you didn't sleep either?"

"I've got this case on my mind," said Tyler. "You might be familiar with it: it involves the death of a sex worker."

"I thought sarcasm was supposed to be my role in this relationship?"

"I'm cutting you some slack. Anyway, I kept thinking about Rayworth."

Mills' eyes widened.

"Not in that way! We may have shared unfortunate upbringings, but I don't see a future for the two of us. No, I was thinking ... bad mouthing Stewart, Trent's boyfriend, or ex boyfriend ... and the young man at Rayworth's flat, Jon Kelly. There's an itch to scratch, I can feel it, though I can't quite name it."

"You want to speak to Kelly?"

"I'm planning to do that, yes. And his last employer too. He worked on the market in Stoke, and it's market day today I understand."

Tyler suddenly leaned forward, adopting an expression suggestive of deep compassion.

"What is it?" asked Mills.

"I don't want to place temptation in your way, Danny. It might be too much too soon. First the supermarket, and now the meat stand at the market."

Mills sneered. "Very funny."

"Okay, if you're quite sure, what are we waiting for?"

*

The market was quiet. It didn't take the detectives long to establish that Fred Wallace, on the meat stall, had been Kelly's recent employer, and that his replacement, a tall, gangly youth with a teddy boy quiff and

85

drainpipes, was happy to look after the stall for five minutes while he went outside with the officers.

Wallace, a large, sweaty faced man in his late forties, shook his head. "They send them from the job centre, and most of them last about a week. But that last one, Kelly, he was a right one."

"In what way?" asked Tyler.

"I think he had the idea that he was here to chat up anything in a skirt. I don't know about employment opportunities; he wasn't the least bit interested in learning a trade. Different kind of opportunity altogether he was after. I couldn't keep him; he was putting the customers off instead of drawing them in. And the last straw was when his girlfriend showed up." Tyler's interest quickened. "He was on his break, and she turns up, asking about him, a dozen questions, customers not impressed – and she had a right mouth on her I can tell you."

"Can you describe her?" said Tyler.

Wallace's description of Kelly's girlfriend fitted Rayworth like a glove.

"She was checking up on him?"

"Sounded like it to me. The sort of Jack the Lad you check up on too. A pair together, I'd say. But once I got rid of lover boy that was it. I haven't seen her again and I'm not complaining, believe me. Anyway, I'd better get back before Teddy Boy scares off any of my remaining customers." Wallace shook his head and laughed. "He might scrub up, it's early days. I try to give them the benefit of the doubt. And I tell you, he can't be any worse than Kelly, that's for sure. I can put up with most things, but once the hand goes in the till, that's that. He denied it, but I had him bang to rights and he knew it. I can tell you to the penny what's in that till at any given time. It's a skill you learn if you want to stay in business, at least in this game.

"I told him he had two choices: either sling his hook, or else we'd make it a police matter. Glad to say I haven't seen him since."

Mills thanked Wallace for his time and the detectives walked back to the car.

"Kelly?" said Mills, and Tyler nodded. "He lives in Fegg Hayes with his parents."

"When he's not at Rayworth's flat. Come on," said Tyler, "it's round the corner, worth a try."

They walked round to the flats and knocked on Rayworth's door. On the third round of knocking the door opened and a groggy Kelly peeped out. "She gone out," he said.

"It's you we'd like to speak to," said Mills.

"Me? What about?"

"Can we come in?"

Kelly looked hesitant, and then shrugged before turning round and letting the detectives follow him into the flat.

The austerity of the place hit Mills for the second time. It was a place to sleep and no doubt to engage in a few other basic activities, and little else. It couldn't be less homely.

"What do you want?" said Kelly.

Tyler said, "Christine's shift ended around midnight on Sunday. Did you see her after work?"

Again Kelly appeared hesitant. "I think so," he said at last. "What day is it now?" He appeared to count the days off on his fingers. "Yes, I was here when she got back."

"And what time was that?"

"I don't keep track of her."

"You were here all evening?" asked Tyler.

"I came over late. I don't know what time. Why do you need to know that?"

"We're investigating the murder of her colleague," said Tyler, and the edge in his voice was unmistakable.

"Nothing to do with me," said Kelly.

"We could continue this down at the station, under caution, if you prefer," said Tyler.

Kelly's grogginess appeared to dissipate, and a new clarity became instantly manifest. "I never know what time she finishes. But it's usually around midnight, on a Sunday, that's if she's working at the West End. So if I'm meeting her here then I aim for around that time."

"You live with your parents in Fegg Hayes," said Mills.

"What's that got to do with anything?"

"Do you drive?"

"What?"

"Taxi?"

"Eh?"

"It's a few miles. Did you drive, or did you get a taxi?"

"I scrounge a lift off my mum."

"Did you know Stacey?" asked Tyler.

"I met her. Anyway, shouldn't you be out trying to catch whoever did it?"

"You say you met her?" said Tyler.

"Once or twice, yes. I didn't really know her though." Tyler kept looking at Kelly. "What?" said Kelly.

"What did you think of her?"

"I didn't think anything."

"You met her through Christine?"

88

"I think I did, yes, probably." Kelly's eyes flashed from one detective to the other.

"When Christine returned to the flat on Sunday night, did she say anything?"

"About what?"

"Anything out of the ordinary, anything about her shift?"

"She didn't talk about work much, and I didn't want to hear about it either. It's none of my business."

"Did either of you leave the flat again on Sunday night?"

"No."

"You are sure about that?" said Tyler. "You might want to think carefully before you confirm what time you arrived at the flat, what time Christine arrived here, and that neither of you left the flat again that night once Christine had returned from work."

Kelly appeared to think it over, and then he said, "I was dropped off here around midnight, Christine got in a bit later, and then we didn't go out again. Will that do?"

"And you *think* you met Stacey through Christine?"

Kelly seemed to be trying hard to maintain the detective's unflinching gaze. "I think so, that's right."

"But you're not sure? You may have met her, what, before you knew Christine?"

"I don't think so."

"Do you know Dean Stewart?"

"I've heard of him. He was Stacey's boyfriend, wasn't he?"

"Have you met him?"

"No."

"How did you hear about him?"

"Through Christine, I think."

"Did she say anything about him?"

"Not much."

"She didn't like him?"

"What is this?" said Kelly.

Tyler went on. "Christine thought Stewart wasn't good for Stacey."

Kelly heard a sound and looked towards the door. "I don't know. Why don't you ask her yourself?"

Tyler turned round to see Rayworth standing in the doorway.

CHAPTER NINETEEN

Their versions tallied. Rayworth and Kelly's account of their movements on Sunday evening suggested that they were both telling the truth, or else conspiring to deceive.

"Kelly was having a relationship with Trent," said Tyler, as the detectives got back in the car. Mills drove back towards Cedar Lane while Tyler continued to ruminate. "Or else Rayworth was seeing Stewart, or possibly both." He was talking in a quiet voice, as though he might have been thinking aloud and not even realising that he was speaking.

When nothing followed the hushed speculations and permutations, Mills said, "Motives for murder, sir?"

"I'd say so, wouldn't you?"

"But ..."

"Spit it out."

"Given that their stories marry up, that would suggest ..."

"Having trouble with your theory, Danny?"

Mills pulled onto the car park at Cedar Lane and gave the matter his full attention. "What I mean is, if there was a motive of jealousy involved, why would either of them cover for the other? It doesn't make sense." He looked across at Tyler. "Does it?"

"It might."

"How?"

"That's what we have to find out."

Mills was shaking his head as he got out of the car.

"You have a better idea?" Tyler asked him.

"I'm afraid I haven't."

Tyler remained seated in the car. "Rayworth and Kelly – they're not going to admit to cheating, and Trent isn't around to ask. So, who does that leave?"

"You mean Stewart?"

"Get back in, Danny. Tea and biscuits will have to wait."

*

Stewart was halfway through his shift at the supermarket when the detectives asked for a word. The supermarket manager, Mr Tideswell, let the detectives use his office, but not before he'd asked questions of his own.

"You suspect Mr Stewart of murder?" asked Tideswell.

"We are at an early stage in our investigations," said Tyler. "We are interviewing a number of people who might have known the victim."

"You are saying that Mr Stewart is *not* a suspect?"

"I'm saying that we would like to ask Mr Stewart a few questions, that's all. But while we're on the subject, did Stacey Trent visit your supermarket?"

"To meet Stewart you mean?"

"For any purpose," said Tyler.

"Not that I'm aware. Of course, she might have come into the store. Despite my considerable work ethic, I don't manage to acquaint myself with every single customer."

"Has Mr Stewart taken any time off lately?"

"Holidays, you mean?"

"Or sick leave, perhaps?"

Tideswell checked the contents of a file extracted from a filing cabinet next to his desk. The information was at his fingertips and he imparted his findings. "Mr Stewart has worked here for eight months, during which time he has taken precisely one week of leave. No sickness absence is indicated. The week's leave was taken just over a month ago."

"No disciplinary issues?" asked Tyler.

"None whatsoever, an exemplary probationary period I would have to say. But I trust that, should you find that he has committed an act of murder whilst in our employment ..."

"You'll be the first to know."

"That is most re-assuring indeed. Then, without further ado, I will summon Mr Stewart and let you get on with your business."

*

Stewart didn't look pleased to see the detectives.

"I've told you all I know about Stacey. We broke up; that's all I can tell you. You're going to get me in trouble if you keep turning up and harassing me like this."

"On the contrary," said Tyler. "Mr Tideswell speaks highly of you. And assisting the police in the execution of their duties can't do any harm to your career prospects."

Tyler's tone appeared to Mills to bear a warning, and was magnified by the DCI's stark expression. "Did you know Christine Rayworth?"

"I met her. She was friends with Stacey."

"Have you seen her recently?"

"She uses this supermarket sometimes, so, yes; she has called in."

"Recently?"

"I couldn't give you the dates."

"But she hasn't called in here to see you?"

"Why would she?"

"You weren't having a relationship with her?"

93

"No."

"Do you know Jon Kelly?"

"No."

Tyler gave a description, and added: "He's Christine Rayworth's boyfriend."

"I don't know him. He doesn't sound familiar."

"Was Stacey seeing anyone after you split up with her?"

"I've no idea. Once we split up, she was nothing to do with me. I have to get back to work now. I don't know anything more about Stacey."

Stewart left the office and a few moments later there came a knock on the door. Mr Tideswell strode back in. "I see that my employee has been allowed to retain his freedom, at least for now."

Tideswell's expression was questioning, but he received nothing further from Tyler to satisfy his curiosity. He thanked Tideswell for the use of his office.

"Anytime, no problem at all," said the manager. "Always a pleasure to assist if we can and in any way that we can. You know where we are. No other of my staff you wish to speak to while you're on the premises?"

Out on the car park Mills said, "He's a bit dry our Mr Tideswell."

"You detected an attitude?" said Tyler.

"I think we're wasting our time here," said Mills.

"Perhaps you are right. But it's not all bad news. I have a meeting with Carstairs in my diary, so there's something to look forward to."

"Always nice to have something to look forward to, sir."

"He will want to know about the progress I am making on the case. It promises to be a brief affair."

"That's the way it goes sometimes, sir."

"Then I'm sure I have nothing to worry about."

*

Mills sat at his desk and assembled all the reports and statements on the case so far. He noticed that Tyler had gone quiet, sitting across from him in mute contemplation. A dark, brooding figure, like the Jim Tyler of old, who lived his life seemingly on a knife edge. Some of that edge had worn down recently, and Mills had been glad of the changes he had witnessed. It was a joy to work with a man like Tyler, a detective full of surprises, and at the same time rock solid when it came to matters of integrity and a natural thirst for justice. But it seemed to Mills that a perfect storm was building once again: A case going nowhere, and pressures bearing down from above in the shape of CS Carstairs, an authority figure if ever there was one, cast in an ancient mould and likely to bring out the very worst in Tyler. *And no woman around to share his troubles with, and to offer consolation on the darkest days.*

He looked up from the mess of statements and reports and caught Tyler's eye. The look startled him.

"I can see the wheels turning, Danny."

Mills smiled uneasily. "You okay, sir?" he asked.

Tyler consulted his watch and stood up. "This can go two ways, in my opinion. It can go badly ... or very badly."

Mills watched him go, and then dug back into his work. It was better to find focus elsewhere than to speculate on events over which he had no control.

CHAPTER TWENTY

Carstairs was sitting behind his desk looking grim-faced. Tyler took his seat opposite and waited.

"The Trent murder," said Carstairs at last. "Update me."

Tyler did as he was bid. It took him less than two minutes.

"Is that it?"

"That's where we're at."

Carstairs employed an old trick, long favoured by high ranking personnel. He glared at his junior colleague with all the intensity he could muster, whilst at the same time sitting stock still and silent. The tactic generally created enough pressure to force the recipient to start talking, in a desperate attempt to call off the dogs.

But Tyler knew the moves too well, and had lost the appetite to give a damn about appeasing whatever ugly bastard happened to by trying to intimidate him. He sat in mirror image to Carstairs, and the silence fermented.

The moments, and then the minutes, ticked by, and at last it was Carstairs who gave in. "You have nothing else to add, DCI Tyler?"

"If I did, I would have done so."

Carstairs almost flinched, and for the first time he began to look flustered. The danger signs were flashing but Tyler had become entrenched; in this kind of mood, in this kind of situation, heaven and hell would fail to move him an inch.

"I want a full report first thing tomorrow, do you understand? And if there are no further developments we may have to take you off the case and re-assign it." Carstairs waited, counting the beats. "You don't have anything further to add?"

"A full report first thing tomorrow," said Tyler. "You'll have it."

Carstairs looked ready to explode, but Tyler held the seething stare and reflected it right back.

"That's it, then. Better let you get on."

Tyler took the cue, stood up and made his way to the door.

"I've heard a lot about you, DCI Tyler, and hear this: I'm not Graham Berkins."

"How's he doing?" asked Tyler.

*

He made his way back to the CID office and sat down. Mills looked up, trying to weigh up from his expression how the meeting had gone. But the poker face was reigning supreme.

"So, sir – badly or very badly?"

"The jury is still out, Danny. But curiously, when I enquired into the health of Berkins, Carstairs seemed to take my concern as a further example of insubordination."

Mills laughed. "Oh dear."

"Quite. What have you been up to in my brief absence?"

"Well, something interesting, actually. I've been putting together a diary of Trent's movements, as far as we can ascertain them, and there appears to be a missing ingredient."

"Tell me more."

"Monday evenings. She never worked Monday evenings, or at least not for some time. I double checked, and I rang Stewart. He's always pleased to hear from us. Anyway, when I asked about it he went quiet, and then he said that was one of the things that had caused the split."

"How do you mean?"

"He knew she didn't work Mondays, and he arranged something one Monday evening, a gig or something that he wanted to take her to, and she said she couldn't make it. That's when he felt she was messing him about, either seeing someone else or just being awkward."

"Did you attempt to narrow it down?"

"He said he just gave up and didn't see her again after that."

"And he never found out about what she was doing with her Monday evenings?"

"That's what he said."

"Do you believe him?"

"It's hard to say. But I'm intrigued to know what she was doing."

"Likewise," said Tyler.

The detectives did the rounds, speaking to Greener at *West End Girls*, Rayworth at her flat in Stoke, before paying another visit to Stewart, who had just started his shift.

Tideswell was on duty at the supermarket and intercepted Tyler and Mills on their arrival, ushering them through to his office. "Here at Sainsbury's we pride ourselves on being the shoplifting capital of the world. Not doing so well when it comes to murder. But things change." He looked pleased with his observation, and clearly prided himself on being something of a comic wit, thought Mills.

But then the manager's expression darkened. "Three visits suggest that you may be onto something. Are you ... closing in?"

It sounded to Mills like a reasonable question. Surely the responsibilities of management extended to ensuring that you were not in the business of retaining staff who might turn out to be cold blooded killers.

"Still routine," said Mills.

"Then I do admire your thoroughness," said Tideswell, evidently still fishing.

"Do you happen to know if Mr Stewart is currently in a relationship?" asked Mills.

"I wouldn't know about that. I'm not aware that he is seeing any of the staff here. It's a small supermarket, and word does get around. There are of course whispers that he was seeing the murdered young woman, and on that account I do have a confession to make. In fact, I was thinking of ringing you, so your visit today is timely."

"Go on," said Mills.

"I spoke to one of our supervisors, Katie; she doesn't miss much, our Katie. And it transpires that Stewart had confided in one of his colleagues to the effect that he had broken up with the woman in question."

"With Stacey Trent, you mean?" said Mills.

"The same, as I understand it, yes."

"Did he think to clarify exactly why he broke up with her?" said Tyler, his tone somewhat impatient.

"Well, reading between the lines," said Tideswell, "it sounds like he'd had enough of being taken for the fool. He was apparently quite disparaging about the young lady, quite *cutting*." Mills winced at the word. If it was intended as a joke, then it was in extreme bad taste. But he gave Tideswell the benefit of the doubt.

99

"In view of what happened to Ms Trent, I wondered if this information might be pertinent."

"In what way?" pressed Tyler.

"Isn't it obvious?" said Tideswell. "If Mr Stewart - who, incidentally, according to Katie, used some rather choice language -"

"What exactly did he say?" asked Tyler his impatience unbridled now.

"From what I've been told, he said something along the lines of ... 'I should have known better than thinking a slag like her could change.'"

"And how long ago was this?"

"Very recently actually, a couple of weeks," said Tideswell, "give or take. I could I'm sure press Katie for a more exact timescale if that would assist with your investigations."

The detectives were once again provided with the use of the manager's office.

"I don't think that this necessarily changes anything," Tyler said to Mills once Tideswell had left them alone. "Even if Stewart was thinking that he was being cheated on ..."

Tyler stopped talking, his features contorted in concentration.

"What is it?" asked Mills.

"We came here today to try to find out what Trent was doing with her Monday evenings."

"We did, sir."

"And nobody else appears to have a clue. But what if Stewart found out?"

There was a knock on the outer door, and Stewart entered the office. He looked angry, belligerent. "Look," he said, "I've told you all I know. I'm going to end up out of a job if you keep -"

"What was Stacey doing on Monday evenings?" asked Tyler.

"How the hell should I know?"

"You imagined that she was seeing someone – that's why she couldn't meet you that Monday evening, when you arranged -"

"I don't care what she was doing, or who she was seeing. I was sick of being let down. So I ended it."

Tyler's eyebrows raised in perfect synchronicity with those of DS Mills.

"What I mean is, I ended the relationship."

"And you expect us to believe that? You weren't curious as to how she was spending the evening?"

"No!"

"Mr Stewart," said Tyler, "I want to know what you found out."

"I don't know what you're talking about."

"Did you follow her? See where she was going, who she was meeting? She was making a fool of you, and you were angry about it. Who was she meeting on Monday evenings, Mr Stewart?"

The belligerence had given way, and Stewart looked pale and worn. "I didn't follow her. I didn't need to." He took a long breath. "You know, I thought that I actually loved her; that we had something special going on. What a laugh! She told me, not long after I first met her, that she was thinking about giving up what she was doing, and going back to college."

Tyler nodded. "Go on."

"She told me how she had enjoyed college to begin with, enjoyed the course she was doing, and then how she met this guy and decided to drop out and follow what she called 'a rock and roll lifestyle'. It was a poke at her parents, too."

"Her parents?" said Tyler.

"She hated them, particularly her father, and she knew it would hurt them, abandoning her studies."

"How would it hurt them?"

"She said they had her life all mapped out: college, university; that just because they had big careers, they thought she had to follow in their footsteps."

"Even though she was enjoying the course?" said Mills.

"She reckoned meeting that guy, Kev, opened her eyes, and she decided to make her own life."

"And came to regret the choices she made?" said Tyler.

"It sounded like it, the way she said it that time. But she was stubborn, pig headed. Everything had to be on her own terms. Even if she liked something, she'd go against it to make a point. I don't think she had a clue what she wanted, not really."

"But she intimated that she was thinking of resuming her studies?" asked Tyler.

"She said it that once. It was like she'd let her guard down. It depended what mood she was in. That's what I couldn't take, because Stacey one day was someone else the next. You didn't know where you stood with her. I didn't want any more of that."

"And did she go back to college - on Monday evenings?"

"That's the thing," said Stewart. "She never mentioned it again. And when I asked her about it, she went all funny with me and told me to back off. And then I asked her another time, and she bit my head off, saying couldn't I accept her for what she was, who she was, and why was I trying to change her, and that I was just like her father. So I didn't bring it up again. And then she started letting me down, and that Monday was the last straw and I told her I'd had enough."

"And what was her response?" asked Tyler.

"She didn't argue and I haven't seen her or spoken to her since."

Tyler looked at the young man, and then turned to Mills. "Any questions you'd like to ask?" When Mills declined they let Stewart get back to his work.

Tideswell came back into his office. "I see that our Mr Stewart is still a free man, at least for the time being. Will you be requiring the use of my office again tomorrow?"

The detectives walked out of the supermarket and Mills drove back, Tyler brooding all the while in the seat next to him. "You alright?" said Mills as they arrived at Cedar Lane.

"Carstairs, despite the lack of evidence, would expect, and might yet demand, an arrest. If I don't do it, he'll get someone else in to do it. So, what have we got: an ex partner, who may well have been ditched by Trent, finds out she's seeing someone else, and takes matters into his own hands?"

"You think that's what happened?"

"If it's good enough for the likes of Carstairs, then it's good enough for me."

"You don't mean that."

"How long have you known me, Danny?"

"Long enough. Look, I can check out the local colleges," said Mills. "See if that's how she was spending her Monday evenings."

"You do that," said Tyler, with an air of nonchalance. "I'll start on my report. And then Carstairs can do what the hell he wants."

103

CHAPTER TWENTY ONE

Tyler wasted no time, and was putting the finishing touches to his report when Mills put the phone down and punched the air. "Stacey Trent was enrolled at Fenton College. She was studying A level psychology."

Tyler looked up. "On a Monday evening?"

"That's the one, sir."

"And she actually attended?"

"I'll firm up on the details this evening."

"Is this your idea of a lifeline?" Tyler tapped the top page of his report. "A ploy to throw some meat into these empty pages?"

"It might not lead us anywhere," said Mills. "But it's something to do."

"This evening, you say?"

"The course tutor is a Geoff Wormsley. He's teaching at the college tonight."

Tyler appeared distracted. Mills began to speak again, when Tyler said, "She was studying A levels originally, with a view to going to university. One A level isn't going to get her far. Fenton College – isn't that where she attended originally?"

"No, that was the one in Shelton, sir."

"Why the switch I wonder. If she was enjoying the course and only dropped out to aggravate her parents, to make a point, or because she was under the influence of the legendary Kev."

*

"Class begins at seven," said Mills as they made their way into reception. "That gives us half an hour." In the reception area he studied the timetable. *Room 7C, main building.*

"Can I help you?" asked a bespectacled librarian of a woman.

"Mr Wormsley's Psychology class," said Mills.

The woman appeared to eye the detectives with suspicion. "Have you enrolled?" she asked.

"Actually, no, we wish to have a quick word with Mr Wormsley."

"Can I help?"

Mills showed his ID. "Do you keep a register of attendance?"

"This is not a high school," the woman said.

"Then we will have to speak to Mr Wormsley after all," said Mills. "Thank you for your help."

They marched across to the main building and found Wormsley setting up the classroom in 7C. He looked up as they entered his domain.

"Can I help you?"

Mills observed that the man had every appearance of a seventies throwback, down to the elbow patches on his tweed jacket and the scruffy jeans that might have cost twice that of a pristine pair. The goatee beard completed the effect, and the voice betrayed an accent of a thorough and privileged education.

Mills made his introduction and asked about Trent.

"Yes, Stacey attended my Monday class," said Wormsley. "How can I help you?"

Over the course of the conversation, the lecturer confirmed that Trent had been a regular attendee and a keen student with a sharp intellect and a notable thirst for knowledge. It sounded to Mills like a standard issue school report, though in truth he'd never achieved one quite so glowing. She had been in attendance the

Monday before her death, and Wormsley told the detectives that he had noted her absence the following week as unusual.

"Did she always arrive alone, leave alone?" asked Tyler.

"I never observed otherwise. She didn't appear to know any of the other students, or to socialise with them during breaks."

"Did you get to know her?"

"Not really. I don't make a habit of getting personal with my students. She contributed to class discussions, and I gave her feedback on essays and assignments, as I do with all my charges. It is an absolute tragedy what has happened, but I'm afraid I can't be of much more help to you."

Students were starting to drift into the classroom.

"Did she arrive late to your class?" asked Mills.

"I don't recall her being late. I believe she was punctual."

"That's not what I meant. She didn't start the course back in September?"

"Oh, I see what you mean. Yes, I believe she did arrive late, in that sense."

"Isn't that rather unusual?"

"I suppose it is, though hardly unheard of."

"It would leave a lot of catching up to do," suggested Mills.

"That's true. But some students have quite a facility when they put their mind to a thing."

"And you would say that she had that facility?"

Wormsley was betraying signs of discomfort. "I really must attend to my students now," he said.

"If anything else occurs to you," said Tyler, "you won't hesitate -"

"Of course."

The detectives made their way out of the building. "Calling it a night?" said Mills.

"Not quite," said Tyler.

Mills followed the DCI back into reception. The librarian woman was daring the two men to approach her for a second time. Tyler wasted not a moment. "I want a list of students attending Mr Wormsley's Monday night A level Psychology class. And I want contact details for all class members. I also want to know when Stacey Trent enrolled, and a comprehensive list of her attendance." His polite smile was not reciprocated. And as far as Mills could detect, he didn't much seem to care either way.

CHAPTER TWENTY TWO

Mills had been tasked with working through the contacts supplied by the college, and Tyler's report was completed and left for the attention of Carstairs. Mills was gnawing away at his fingers in between making phone calls, Tyler watching him like a hawk. At last Mills looked up. "Not much doing," he said. "But there are a couple of potentially interesting ones, possibly three."

"Let's be generous," said Tyler. Then he said, "Haven't you eaten today, I mean apart from skin and nails?"

"My appointment's today. 5pm."

"Hoping to lose another stone through sheer hard police work?"

Mills didn't respond to that, and looked back at his list. "I've arranged to see Kate Lewis and Martin Brownsword this morning. Lewis actually asked for a face to face, and Brownsword seems to have taken a dislike to his teacher."

"There was someone else?"

"Georgina Lowry. She didn't say much at all."

"Making her the most intriguing of all."

"Something like that."

"I'd say go for it. Trust those instincts of yours why don't you. I've not heard back from Carstairs as yet, so while I'm still on the case I'm paying another visit to our old friend Eric Faron. He's been back outside *The Sweet Box*, making his presence felt. Greener reckons he's started making comments to some of the girls as they enter and leave the premises."

Mills put his jacket on.

"Good luck at the doc's," said Tyler. "And sorry about my dig earlier, I'm teetering for some reason, can't think why. Missing Berkins no doubt. I hear they're operating on him later."

"I didn't know that," said Mills. Then: "You alright, Jim?"

"More or less. Possibly I've come to rely on Berkins too much; too weak to fend for myself. If it comes to it, I'm not sure I'm up for another fight. If Carstairs has any instinct for the job at all, he will smell my weakness and pick me off at his leisure. But don't let me keep you."

*

Kate Lewis turned out to be a time waster, the sort who liked the attention of a detective coming to her flat asking questions. She had nothing to give in return apart from some cheap gossip about other course members and their petty indiscretions. Mills kicked himself for not picking all that up over the phone, and he cut the visit short.

Martin Brownsword was a different prospect, and he was gunning for Wormsley.

"I only stick the course because I need the qualification this year. My CV's a bit thin for what I'm doing, and what I hope to be doing."

Brownsword, an intense, skinny young man with thick spectacles and a nervous twitch, had added a night class to his full time college course, and he was paying the rent working at a mental health hostel in the city. He looked like he was short of sleep, a decent meal, and a life that was worth living.

"What don't you like about Mr Wormsley?"

In the gospel according to Martin Brownsword, Wormsley spent too much time flirting with the young women in the class, and trying to show off his intellect with vulgar displays that were of no help whatsoever to his more serious students.

And if nothing else, thought Mills, Brownsword was most certainly in the category marked 'serious'. He wondered when the young man had last smiled, or even laughed. But he remembered Stacey Trent. He'd never actually spoken to her, didn't seem the type to have ever spoken with a presentable young woman in his entire life, yet he'd noticed the way Wormsley interacted with her.

"Are you suggesting a relationship?" asked Mills.

"I wouldn't be surprised."

"You don't have any evidence that they were actually seeing each other outside of the course?"

Mills watched Brownsword carefully. The young man was giving the impression that a valuable opportunity was slipping away. That he would have loved nothing more than to have backed up his speculations with some incontrovertible facts, and seen Wormsley go down for murder. Yet in the end nothing was forthcoming; and either Brownsword lacked the wit or the nerve to fabricate a scenario that might lead to the lecturer's fall, or else he bottled it.

Georgina Lowry lived with her parents in a detached property in Trentham. She had said very little over the phone, but Mills had sensed that something was lurking in the shadows. She was a small, neat, cagey young woman, and like Brownsword she was supplementing a full time college course with an evening class in Psychology. Her parents were out earning the mortgage, which, looking at the house, Mills imagined would be substantial, entailing considerable time at the coal face quite possibly, whilst affording their daughter plenty of peace and quiet to get on with her studies.

She spoke a lot less than Martin Brownsword did, but eventually she made similar observations, particularly in regard to Wormsley's interactions with some of his female students.

Stacey Trent? Mills asked, and Lowry nodded at mention of the name, and then lowered her eyes as though as a mark of respect. She was one of the students Wormsley had 'interacted' with, though not the only one.

Then it came out. Lowry had a friend, Caroline, and she attended the same class; Wormsley made a pass, discreetly, Caroline declined the advance and kept it to herself. Then it happened a second time, one week when Lowry didn't attend, seizing his opportunity, his hand on her shoulder down by the coffee machine, Caroline leaving the college that night and never returning.

"She told me about it a few weeks later. I kept asking her why she had left the course. I was beginning to wonder. I'd seen how Wormsley was with one or two of the women, and in the end she told me what happened. I told her to make a complaint but she wouldn't. I said I was going to leave the course but Caroline said I mustn't do that. She made me promise. I've kept my eye on him since then. I don't like him and I don't trust him."

Another one who would like to see Wormsley rot in prison for murder, thought Mills.

Attendance records showed that Trent had come late to the course, possibly the week after Lowry's friend Caroline had been approached for the second time.

Lowry couldn't remember the exact sequence but agreed it was around that time.

"How was he with Stacey?" asked Mills.

"Well, it was kind of weird. Sometimes ... I would watch her sitting there, just staring at him. It was like something was going on but I wasn't sure what it was."

Mills left Lowry to her studies. He sat in his car processing the recent conversations, before starting up the engine.

CHAPTER TWENTY THREE

The outer door of *The Sweet Box* was open for business, and Tyler rang the bell. A dark haired woman with more attitude than clothing opened the door and gave him a toothy smile. Then she turned around with a flourish and he followed her inside.

A long corridor, similar to the one at West End stretched down between a line of closed doors. "Hayley Greener's expecting me," he said.

The woman grinned back at him over her shoulder and pointed to a door on the left. Tyler knocked, and a familiar voice invited him in. He watched the dark haired woman mince her way down the corridor, and for a moment he was lost. Then he pressed down on the handle and entered the room.

The office was even more compact than the one at *West End Girls*, the room chaotic, the stale odour of sex seeming to pervade through the walls and floors. Or maybe it was his imagination. He conceded the possibility.

Greener looked up from making notes and thanked him for coming over.

"Having trouble with our old friend?" said Tyler.

"He's unsettling my girls. I want something doing. After what happened to Scarlet – *Stacey* – they're getting nervous as hell. Two of the girls haven't come in today. There must be something in the air."

He asked her what she meant by that.

"Stan Baker's got heavy handed again with one of the girls. And over at *West End* that Hately guy's been asking to see Scarlet again. He's been in twice already today; that's never right. He gives me the creeps, so what with him and Baker and this basket case outside - can't you do something?"

"Who hasn't turned up?" asked Tyler.

"Well, Phillipa, for one. That jerk outside blew her a kiss when she was leaving yesterday, and he was making obscene gestures at her when she walked past him. He's getting worse. She said she won't come in again until you've sorted him out. And Christine ..."

"She hasn't turned in for the same reason?"

"I assume that's the reason."

"You haven't asked her?"

"I haven't got hold of her yet. It's not like her, but that pervert is affecting all my staff; it can't go on, we don't know what he's capable of."

"You don't hire security?"

"Do me a favour! They cause more trouble than the punters most of the time."

"When was Christine last in?"

"Yesterday. And that dick out there had a go at her when she came in. It must have unsettled her because she wasn't herself all day. I've not seen her like that. He's started doubling his shifts. I tell you, something's going to happen. I don't like the look of that pervert, not one bit."

"He wasn't outside when I came in," said Tyler.

"Perhaps he knew you were coming."

"And trouble with Baker and Hately: are you sure you don't need some security?"

"They're old men, when all's said and done. But Baker slapped Chloe and she's threatening to walk off if it happens again. As for Hately – he's driving them mad, I mean, turning up asking for Scarlet twice a day ..."

The phone on Greener's desk rang and she answered it. While she was talking Tyler caught a sound from outside the door; he opened it and looked out. The dark haired woman was standing outside in the corridor. She grinned at the DCI.

"What's your name?" he asked.

"May."

"Have you got five minutes?"

"I've got five for you," she said, and led him down the corridor and into one of the other rooms.

The room was small, containing a bed, two chairs and little else. "You've been having fun around here, I believe?" he said.

"That loser outside, you mean?"

"You knew Stacey?"

"I knew her. She was alright."

"Christine?"

"I don't like Christine. I never did."

"Any reason?"

"She plays games."

"She'd get on well with Ted Freely then by the sound of things."

"He's harmless enough, if you know how to handle him. But I wouldn't call Christine harmless."

"What are you saying, May?"

"Don't get me wrong, I'm not pointing the finger. I'm not saying she killed Stacey."

"Then what are you saying?"

"I keep my eyes and ears open, that's all."

"And what have you seen, what have you heard?"

"Kelly had a thing with Stacey, for one thing. And they were trying to get money out of some teacher Stacey reckoned had 'cradle-snatched' her at college. That's a laugh."

"What is?"

"Stacey could always take care of herself. She was a big girl. She didn't get into anything she couldn't handle."

"It seems that she *couldn't* take care of herself, in view of what happened. So what don't you like about Christine, then?"

"Well, how about she stole my boyfriend."

"Jon Kelly?"

"That's him. She sees anyone with something and she wants it."

"He seems a popular choice around here," said Tyler.

"Some men have that thing," she said.

"There isn't more to it than that?"

The door swung open and Greener was standing there. "This looks cosy," she said. "Telling tales again, May?"

"Only true ones. Christine hasn't come in because Jon's dumped her."

"The trouble with murder investigations," said Tyler, "they don't leave time in the day for settling domestic disputes."

Greener's jaw dropped as Tyler made his way out.

There was still no sign of Eric Faron out on the street.

*

Mills sat in the waiting room running it through his head. Wormsley was the Psychology teacher at Shelton College when Trent was attending, and had more recently taken up the post of lecturer at Fenton College. Was it coincidence that Trent found herself back in Wormsley's class, or had she chosen it that way? And if so, why would she do that? Did she rate him that highly? There was an A level Psychology class running in Shelton one evening a week. Perhaps, having left that college once, she felt awkward about returning, and wanted a fresh start. But a fresh start with the same lecturer? Wormsley hadn't mentioned that he had known Trent from his time at Shelton. Was that significant?

Mills was startled at the sound of his name being called, and followed the nurse through to the consulting room.

She was a business-like woman with strong auburn hair and freckles, thin as a rake, and he'd already caught her glancing with disdain at the dome of his belly.

Exercise: Getting out of bed and climbing the stairs to get back into it.

The joke didn't even raise a smile.

Smoking/drinking: Not guilty, and guilty. But cutting down, only on match days, and home games at that, amounting to a couple of pints down at the Britannia Stadium every other week, and maybe the odd pint here and there and ...

Another look of disdain and the requirement of a weekly total to add into the box on the form, which he underestimated, of course, and he could see that she knew it. Standard practice, no doubt.

Diet: Much improved, thanks to his wife, though recent lapses could not be denied.

Stress: Working as a detective sergeant.

The scales: his weight up, his belly looking suitably ashamed as it wobbled in disgrace under his shirt, fooling nobody.

Blood pressure: not bad for his age.

Conclusions: more exercise and a far stricter diet.

Any questions: "Are meat pies out of the question?"

A diet sheet supplied, and a look from the nurse as she handed it over, a look that suggested she had just wasted valuable minutes of her working life and fully expected the diet sheet to end up in the bin on the way out. A man sent in by his wife; a hopeless case who would no doubt end up on the cardiac ward in due course. Next!

*

Tyler pulled up outside the home of Jon Kelly in Fegg Hayes, a few miles from *The Sweet Box.* The house was a corner terrace and the front looked close to derelict. Kelly opened the door and he bore the clear scars from a recent altercation. A shrill voice from behind Kelly, a woman's voice, shouted, "Who is it?"

Kelly asked Tyler what he wanted.

"Just a few questions regarding Stacey Trent."

"I've told you what I know," said Kelly.

Then the woman appeared in the doorway standing next to Kelly. She was small, withered, probably late thirties but old before her time, a cigarette in the corner of her mouth that jerked up and down as she talked. "You the police, you look like it? Saw enough of your type when my old man was still around. What you been up to, Jon?" Then she laughed and shook her head. "You seen what she's done to him, the mad bitch? Is that why you're here? She wants locking up and throw away the key!"

Kelly had bruising around his right eye and a swollen lip.

"Your girlfriend assaulted you?" Tyler asked Kelly.

Kelly told him how Rayworth had accused him of being unfaithful. That she was always accusing him.

118

That she had accused him of having a relationship with Trent.

"I'd like you to make a formal statement," said Tyler.

"She wants banging up," said the woman. "What she's done to my Jon."

Tyler asked her where she was last Sunday evening.

"What's that got to do with anything?"

"I'm investigating a murder that took place -"

But even before he could finish the sentence, she said, "Oh, Sunday night – I was running Jon over to see that mad fucker." She glanced at her son, as though the gesture might go unnoticed.

"And what time would that have been?" asked Tyler.

"I'd say it was around midnight. Yes, definitely midnight, I remember now."

"I see," said Tyler. Remarkable memory, he thought. "And where did you drop Jon off?"

"What? At her flat, of course, where else?"

"And where would that be?"

"What? In Stoke."

"Can you be more precise?"

She was trying very hard not to glance again at her son. At last she said, "Oh, I don't know. He got out in Stoke. I haven't got time to fanny about with that one way system, so I dropped him in the town centre. He's a big boy now."

Neatly saved thought Tyler.

At Cedar Lane Kelly made a statement. According to him, Rayworth was bitter and twisted, and jealous of Trent. She threatened him that if she ever found out he was unfaithful she would kill him. Did he believe the threat was credible? Kelly said that he believed it was.

Did he think she was capable of murder? Yes, she was capable even of that.

He asked Kelly if he knew anything about how Trent had spent her Monday evenings lately, and Kelly shrugged. He wasn't having an affair with her; didn't know anything of her personal life.

Tyler found Rayworth in her flat. There were no visible marks of violence on her, at least not on the parts of her body that were exposed when she answered the door to the detective.

"He's been telling tales, has he? Well, he got what he deserved for mucking me about."

"You believe that Kelly was having an affair?"

"I don't just believe it, I *know* it."

"Do you know who the affair was with?"

"He has loads of them, it's how he is. He's a fucking animal."

"Was he having an affair with Stacey?"

"Probably." Then she looked at Tyler and waved a finger at him. "Oh, no you don't! I see where you're going – he thinks – that bastard's trying to say I killed Stacey? He's a low-down scum bag, he really is. I shouldn't be surprised he'd sink to that. He's vicious, you know, he's a liar and a bully."

"A bully?"

"Controlling, you name it, subtle threats, and I've had the odd slap over my time with him. He's no fucking angel and no victim either."

"You still maintain that you returned to your flat on Sunday night, after your shift ended at *West End Girls*? And that you met Kelly here?"

"He's tried to say that's not what happened?"

"Is that what happened?" Tyler asked.

She seemed to be weighing something up. There was almost a twinkle in her eye when she said, "But I was back here first. He came in after me. Can he account for what he was doing on his way over here?"

"His alibi suggests he was dropped here around midnight."

"Alibi? You mean his mother? She runs him around, and when she doesn't she'll say she does, anything to protect her precious Jon. You don't believe a word she tells you."

"Are you suggesting," said Tyler, "that Jon was meeting Stacey?"

"He could have been. I wouldn't be surprised. I wouldn't say you could trust either of them. I'm sorry what happened to her, of course I am, and I used to like her. But she got around, if you know what I mean, and if there was a bloke on tap she took a fancy to, she couldn't help herself."

"Are you – do you believe that she was having a relationship with Jon Kelly? That she saw him, arranged to meet him that night and -"

"Anything's possible," she said. "And the more I think about it ..."

*

Mills left the clinic at half past five and drove to Clayton, just out of the city. Featherstone Drive was a cul de sac of old semis, no more than a couple of dozen of them, substantial properties tucked discreetly away from the main arteries and thoroughfares.

He parked outside a property halfway along, the shabbiest of them all, with a tired looking Honda Accord parked outside that looked in need of directions to the nearest scrap yard, and assistance to get there.

121

Geoff Wormsley opened the front door on the third round of knocking.

The inside of the house looked as tired as the outside, but Wormsley was keeping up some standards, at least where his fashion sense was concerned, with designer jeans and a roll neck sweater that might have been cashmere.

Mills took a seat in the spacious, dingy lounge, and Wormsley sat opposite.

"How can I help you?" he asked.

There was a charm about the man, a suave quality that appeared effortless, though Mills suspected that it might quickly prove wearing.

"I understand that you used to teach at Shelton College?"

"That's correct. I was there for many years, actually. I might have been there now had a better opportunity not arisen a few miles up the road."

"More money?"

"Sounds pathetic when you put it as bluntly as that. But we all have bills to pay, as I'm sure you can appreciate only too well. Naturally, there was a little more to it than that; life isn't all about the money, after all. I got a little frustrated at the ethos at Shelton: the machinery of business and all that; less about the academic, more about securing funding and ticking boxes. The philosophy at Fenton, on the other hand -"

Mills had already had enough. "You taught Stacey Trent?"

"I thought that we had already established as much. She attended my evening class on a -"

"You knew her previously," said Mills.

The flick of an eye; the tilt of the head. "Ah, actually that is true. After so many years doing this job ... so many thousands of students ... but, yes, you are right."

"She was a student at Shelton College?"

"She was, though I'd be hard pressed to name the year."

Mills' dislike of the man was rising. "You didn't remark on the fact that she had been your student before?"

"Remark? I'm sorry, I'm not sure what – you mean to you and your colleague? Like I said, I have seen so many students over the years."

"I mean to her. She didn't recognise you, or you recognise her, and comment on the fact?"

"I don't recall doing so. She might have looked familiar. I really don't know."

"And yet you now recall that you did previously teach her, and that she attended your class at Shelton."

Mills could see the cracks appearing; Wormsley's articulation faltering. He knew what he meant but couldn't quite seem to frame it.

Wormsley waited to see what else the detective might have up his sleeve, and Mills could see what the man was doing. There was an ace card to play; it was right there in Wormsley's eyes, the fear of what revelations were in store.

"You didn't have much to do with her at Shelton?"

Wormsley appeared to relax; sensing that he was off the hook. It was as though a long and silent breath had been released into the room, and Mills felt it sweep by him.

"Like I said, thousands of students, and very few of them stand out. I'm afraid that she must have been one of the many, sad to say, *unremarkables*."

Mills drove away, and all the time something was nagging away at him. If there was a history between Trent and Wormsley ... is that why she returned to college?

As Mills passed through Cheadle and out beyond into the deepening countryside, thoughts of the case receded, to be replaced with the prospect of returning home and the inevitable interview that lay ahead.

CHAPTER TWENTY FOUR

What do you buy a man who has just undergone surgery for stomach ulcers? Probably not grapes and chocolates, concluded Tyler as he called at the Tesco Express on his way to the hospital.

He left the forecourt with a handful of flowers. It was, according to the philosophers, always the thought that counted.

CS Graham Berkins was one in a million. He had taken Tyler on when doubtless not another chief super in the country would have touched him with a barge pole. Striking a senior officer; a reputation as a maverick officer hard to manage, with a drink problem on top; and yet Berkins hadn't flinched, had cut him the slack he needed, and recognised good detective work when he saw it, and integrity beyond any doubt when it was staring him in the face. Without Berkins, Tyler knew that his career would have been in tatters, and there were still many who, knowing him, either in person or by reputation, would be glad to see him fall.

The likes of Carstairs, for instance. It couldn't hurt the CV of a man like Carstairs to bring down the black sheep, and show any other aspiring mavericks out there the consequences of not towing the line. Carstairs wouldn't be happy until he had reached the very top, and that meant treading with full weight on anything beneath him that didn't chime to the notes in his repertoire.

Berkins was sitting up in bed at the end of a long ward. When he saw Tyler approaching with a floral tribute, he looked about to burst into tears or laughter. It was a tough call.

"I didn't know you cared," he said.

"I don't. These are on behalf of the department. I just happen to be the unlucky guy in the sweep. How's it going?"

"I understand it was a good op," said Berkins, moving a shade gingerly in his bed in search of a more comfortable position. "We'll see what the consultant has to say. How's the case progressing?"

"Slowly."

"I imagine Carstairs is on your back."

"Less so than I expected, actually." Tyler looked at the flowers in his hand. "I could do with a vase or something."

"Not used to buying flowers, are you?"

"It shows? You'd prefer lilies?"

"I hate lilies. They signify death. I intend to return to haunt you in *this* life. But you look like a man trying to dump a wasps' nest. Mrs B will be here shortly. She'll know what to do."

Tyler placed the flowers on the table next to the chief superintendant, and sat in the chair next to the bed. "Good to see you looking so well," he said. "But I won't wear you out."

"It's good of you to visit, Jim. I take it this is a social call?"

"I wouldn't talk shop to a man who has just been under the knife."

"I don't know what else we would talk about. So, come on, that case intrigues me. What do you know?"

Tyler told him about Rayworth, the boyfriends, the peculiar clients, the psychology teacher, and the previous owner of one of the establishments Stacey Trent had worked in.

"But no evidence?"

"And no alibis for any of them. Take your pick, or else start again from scratch."

"What do your instincts say, Jim?"

"They don't."

"You don't think it's anyone on the radar so far?"

"I just don't know. I'm out of ideas. We need a break, something to fall into place or come out of the blue. Otherwise we'll keep going around in circles, getting nowhere."

Berkins nodded, knowingly. "That's why Carstairs is backing off."

"He blames me for giving you ulcers."

Berkins laughed and then winced. "No jokes, please, Jim. Doctor's orders."

"You think I'm joking?"

"Not really. Don't give him ammunition. Play by the book. If he thinks I'm not coming back, he'll step things up. But he's no fool. He'll always do what's best for his beautiful career. Remember that."

"It's seared into my brain."

"You look tired, Jim, and I'd have to say a little frazzled. A case like this will do that. Go home and get some rest. You'll get that break, or else fall asleep one night and wake up with the solution screaming at you. Carstairs will have to cut you more slack than he'll let on, he has little choice."

"Let's hope so."

*

Mills walked into the house and his wife was waiting. "How did it go, Danny?"

The inquisition was about to begin.

127

"Is this a formal interview?" he asked.

"Don't be like that."

"What are the kids up to?"

"And don't try to change the subject. They're doing their homework. You have my undivided attention."

"That's what I'm worried about."

"So, how did you go on?"

He took a seat at the table and spilled the beans.

"Did you draw up an action plan, with clear goals?"

"I did indeed," said Mills. "An extra pint on match days and pies all the way to the grave."

"Danny, be serious."

"Lose three stone for starters and take regular exercise."

"What exercise did you have in mind?"

He licked his lips and tried to adopt a smooth tone. "Well," he said. "I thought we might make a start later this evening. Work up a sweat – I'm not saying it's going to be easy but needs must."

"Danny, will you please be -"

"I've never been more serious in my life. But I know that regular *relations* – that's only part of the answer. I thought about joining the local baths, or the gym as a last resort."

"Why don't you ask Jim Tyler if you can join him for a run one evening?"

"He's practically an Olympic athlete!"

"I'm sure he'd go easy on a beginner."

"What's for tea?"

"Danny, will you -"

"I've still got to eat."

Mills' home exercise regime did not kick in that evening, as he had hoped that it might. And once the light in the bedroom had gone out he lay on his side of the bed, reflecting on the case; he was thinking of Geoff Wormsley as he finally fell asleep.

Back in the heart of the city, in the ancient doomsday village of Penkhull, Tyler likewise lay in the darkness, his mind roaming over the case. His focus was on Rayworth, and Kelly, and Stewart; the configurations, the variations; trying to make something fit. He was thinking of CS Berkins when he at last found sleep, and not for the first time counted his blessings in finding a senior officer who wasn't bent on breaking him down or else throwing him to the dogs.

As Tyler and Mills rested in their respective beds, something else was waiting to explode, something that would surprise both of them and in equal measure.

CHAPTER TWENTY FIVE

Val Hackett had been at the hairdressers, her old friend Margaret Swithin giving her the works. The salon had been empty most of the afternoon, and so the two friends had enjoyed something of a catch up while the perm was applied along with the colouring and the styling. It was long overdue, and Hackett had decided that it was time to move on. She insisted on emerging from the salon a new woman.

And then the mood had changed. Talk of moving on had given way to morbid recollections of her late husband, and then caustic remarks had arisen about the brothel and its owner and employees who were trashing Phil's memory with their filthy business.

Some of the remarks had gone beyond caustic, had in fact gone a good way beyond, and Margaret Swithin had herself lain in her bed that night, playing over her recollection of the conversation – no, at that point, not a conversation at all, more a rant, a dark, seething promise of retribution.

Swithin had got out of bed early that morning, believing that she hadn't slept at all, and still trying to decide whether she ought to speak to somebody about what her friend had said.

Would it be a betrayal to do that, or her duty? Val had become so angry, her words feeding on themselves and whipping up a storm, something of a frenzy; what if she needed help? What if she was still deeply grieving for her beloved husband and grief was taking a toll on her health and well being? It was her public duty and it was her duty as a friend, too.

With this in mind, she picked up the phone and rang the local police station; when they put her through, she found herself speaking to DS Mills.

The call was ending when Tyler strode into the office, instantly catching the look on the face of the DS. "Everything alright?".

"An interesting call about Val Hackett, sir."

"*How* interesting?"

"She told her hairdresser that she was planning to burn *The Sweet Box* down."

"Let's go," said Tyler.

*

Val Hackett answered the door and she looked pleased to see the detectives, as though two old friends had been kind enough to interrupt their doubtless busy schedules on her account. She invited them inside and wasted no time in boiling the kettle and setting up a tray with hot drinks and biscuits. Once everyone was seated and the drinks and nibbles distributed, she asked how she might help.

Mills looked across at Tyler, and felt nothing but relief when the DCI took it upon himself to do the explaining. When he had finished, Hackett sat back in her seat and said, "I see." Then she selected a biscuit, and munched on it thoughtfully, washing it down with a mighty gulp from her cup of tea. "Where are my manners?" she said, picking up the plate and pushing it towards the detectives, who both politely declined, though Mills did so with something of a sorrowful look on his face, for the plate included many of his favourites. But sacrifices, he knew, came with the role of detective sergeant; the moment, the situation, wasn't right, and acceptance of further hospitality seemed to him to compromise his position. He waited for Tyler or Hackett to speak. In the event it was Hackett.

"It seems that was said in private has been repeated publicly," she said. "I would have thought that all the years I have known Margaret would have counted for something."

"I think," said Tyler, "that she was concerned for you."

"Concerned? She needn't be. I'm not mad. I'm not about to top myself."

"You spoke of planning to burn down a property," said Tyler.

Silence descended on the room, and it was Mills who broke it. "Sometimes we say things in the heat of the moment, things that we don't really mean. We say things because, well, we're upset, angry ..."

Hackett was shaking her head.

Mills ran out of words and Hackett again offered him the biscuit plate. This time he accepted, taking a milk chocolate hobnob and a custard cream: an almost impossible choice. It felt, somehow, like the least that he could do, and she appeared to smile at the kindness of the gesture.

"I didn't say those things in the heat of the moment; I said them because I meant them. The owner of that ... that *place* ... and those vile creatures who work there, they soil the memory of my beloved Phil and they should burn in hell. I planned to set fire to that wretched abomination, to burn it to the ground. I had every intention of doing so."

"What stopped you?" asked Tyler.

"Shall I tell you? Would you like to hear the truth, so you can get the full measure of me? What stopped me was I didn't have the nerve. I didn't have the courage to

132

do what was right and to make them pay." Her eyes were misting. "I let my Phil down because I didn't have the courage of my convictions, and if I did then I would have set fire to that evil place and with all of them inside.

"There, I've said it!"

"You don't mean that," said Mills.

"Don't I?"

"Mrs Hackett, did you kill Stacey Trent?" asked Tyler.

Hackett looked stunned, shaken; she swallowed the rest of her tea and glared back at the DCI.

"*Mrs Hackett?*"

At last her unblinking eyes gave way to tears. But still she didn't answer the question.

Tyler gestured to Mills, and taking him out of the room, he whispered, "Greener has suggested that threats have been made, including anonymous ones to burn the property down unless they cease trading."

The detectives returned into the room. Hackett was wiping her eyes, but when she looked at Tyler her expression was one of anger. "My precious Phil gave his life, the best years of his life, to that shop; he loved that business - and look what they have done to it. They are trash; they don't deserve to be called human beings."

"Mrs Hackett," said Tyler, "did you attack Stacey Trent?"

Again Hackett refused to answer.

Tyler took care of the formalities, reading the woman her rights, before taking her away.

CHAPTER TWENTY SIX

In the presence of a duty solicitor Tyler and Mills asked Hackett questions for over an hour, and she maintained her silence throughout. The threats that she had apparently made had been to burn the building down, and not to murder individuals who were employed there. And yet she still refused to deny the charge that she had attacked Stacey Trent, and failed to provide an alibi for the time that Trent was killed.

The solicitor asked for a comfort break for his client and privacy to speak with her. The detectives left the interview room and headed up to the CID office.

"Thoughts?" said Tyler.

Mills was checking his messages. Two former students from Shelton College had come forward with the suggestion that Wormsley had affairs with some of his students, including Trent. Both were happy to speak to the DS.

"I don't know what to make of it," said Mills. "I'd say she's making a stand."

"But what kind of a stand?"

"I think she's making threats, but I don't imagine her actually carrying them out. And I certainly don't see her following Trent to the lido and slashing her with a knife."

"Stranger things have happened," said Tyler.

"That's true enough."

"Grief can change a person. It can do strange things even to kindly retired sweet shop owners."

"I don't doubt it. But I still don't see her cutting a young woman's throat and slashing her face to pieces."

Mills told Tyler about the most recent messages.

"Ah," said Tyler. "Now we're talking. Psychology teachers are a different breed altogether. The teaching profession in general, in my experience. But throat cutting and face slashing psychologists ... altogether more credible, wouldn't you say?"

"I think I ought to at least hear what these former students have to say, sir."

"Why wouldn't you, we're not getting anywhere with our aspiring arsonist. Make your arrangements and I'll see if the brief has been able to work any magic down there."

While Mills made phone calls, Tyler went back to the interview room.

*

Alison Goocher had completed her A levels but decided against going to university. She was living at home with her mother, and looking to increase the hours she was currently working at the care agency.

"Mum's getting forgetful, so there are things to do here," she told Mills in the front room of the terraced house in Hanley, a stone's throw from Cedar Lane. "But I remember Stacey. She stood out; she was a character, a bit glamorous, and very attractive. I didn't really know her, but you couldn't help noticing when she was around."

"Alison!"

The voice was coming from the next room.

"Just excuse me a minute, please." The young woman went through to the living room and returned a few minutes later, smiling and shaking her head. "Mum gets a bit panicky. We lost dad last year, and I don't think she's ever got over it."

"I'm sorry to hear that," said Mills.

"Just one of those things. We'll be alright. I had thought about uni; I got some good grades. But I can't see it happening now."

The sound of coughing from next door caused the young woman to pause for a moment. Once the coughing had stopped she said, "Anyway, you wanted to know about Wormsley."

"What was he like?"

"I'd say he was another character. He was a bit creepy, to be honest, but he was a good teacher. I got my best grades in his class. He knew how to put something over, make it memorable and vivid; he made it come alive somehow."

"You mentioned that he was 'a bit creepy'?"

"I didn't like being on my own with him. He had that look about him, and a reputation, too."

"A reputation?"

"Having affairs with students he took a fancy to."

"And Stacey was one of his affairs?"

"I think so, yes. There were rumours about them seeing each other. But then she was seeing this lad, he wasn't in any of my classes. He was very striking, and I knew he was in a band, and he and Stacey seemed to be an item, and then she left the course."

"You didn't see her again after that?"

"No, I never did. And then I heard about what happened, and I remembered the name, and there was a photograph of her, and you couldn't forget a face like that."

A face like that, thought Mills. All that prettiness and character carved up in one savage attack.

"One of the other girls on my course, Rachel, she knew her better than I did."

"That would be Rachel Knightly?"

"Rachel reckoned she walked in on them one time."

"Walked in on them?"

"You know ..."

The sound of coughing once again issued from next door, and again Alison paused to listen until the fit had passed. "I'll just go and check on her again, if that's okay."

Mills was wondering how Tyler was getting on back at the station, when the young woman returned into the room. "I need to pop out to the chemist in a bit."

"I won't keep you. You were saying ..."

"Oh, yes, about Rachel. She'd gone back to the classroom for something, and when she walked in, thinking the room was empty, Wormsley and Stacey were at the back, and they parted quickly and had that look of being, you know, *interrupted.* So Rachel was convinced that they were having an affair."

"Did Rachel tell you anything else?"

"Not really. She asked me if I thought she ought to report something like that."

"And did you?"

"We only talked about it that one time. I think we decided that they were both grownups, and so it was their own business. It's not like if you're at school, is it. I mean, she was old enough to make her own mind up. But every time I saw Wormsley after that I couldn't help but think about it. And Rachel left the course a few weeks later."

"Did you keep in contact?"

"Not really. I saw Rachel a couple of times, knocking around, and I asked her if that was why she left college. It seemed such a coincidence, I suppose. But she never said that was the reason she left. I've often wondered though."

"*Alison!*"

"Sorry, I'd better see to her, and get down to the chemist. I hope I've been helpful."

*

Hackett had broken her silence. Tyler listened intently while the duty solicitor looked on.

"Do you know that last week would have been our wedding anniversary?"

"What day was that?" asked Tyler.

Hackett laughed: a bitter sound. "No, it wasn't what you think it was. It wasn't on the day that woman was murdered. I didn't further soil my sweet dear husband's memory by going out and doing something as obscene as that."

"You didn't kill Stacey Trent?"

"The police have done nothing about that filthy whorehouse!"

"So why should you help us with our enquiries?"

She pointed at the solicitor. "He talked sense into me. I've made my point, but it helps no-one if I get arrested for killing somebody and let the murderer get away with it. I haven't killed anybody. But that place wants closing down, it's a disgrace, I tell you. And I'll tell you something else while I'm about it: I won't stop until something's done."

*

Mills drove over to his old stomping ground in the east of the city, and parked up on Longton Old Road close to the police station where he had once worked the beat.

Rachel Knightly was waiting on the doorstep. She placed a finger up to her lips and then pointed up to the bedroom above. When Mills had cleared the threshold she closed the door quietly behind him.

Once inside the house, in a small living room at the rear of the house, she said, "He's working nights. And boy does he need his beauty sleep."

Mills smiled and took a seat.

"Would you like a drink?"

He couldn't say no. With a mug of strong tea in his hand, he made a start. "You remember Stacey Trent?"

Knightly talked at length and in detail, and in slightly hushed tones, of her time at Shelton College. She, like her friend Alison, thought that Geoff Wormsley was a bit creepy, though a decent enough teacher. "Mind you, I wouldn't have fancied too many one to ones with him."

She described, as her friend had done, how she had stumbled across them "having a snog or a good grope or maybe both. They didn't half jump though when they saw me coming through that door." She also recalled Stacey having a boyfriend who was in a band at the time. "I thought he looked a bit of a prick to be honest. Trying a bit hard to be Mr Cool. But Stacey was always a bit larger than life, how she dressed and that, her hair and make–up. They suited each other, very rock and roll."

"I understand that Stacey dropped out of the course early," said Mills.

"She did, yes. There were rumours ..."

Mills edged forward in his seat. "What rumours?"

"It wasn't long after that time I saw them together – Stacey and Wormsley I mean. This boyfriend was hanging around -"

Mills waved a hand. "Whoa," he said, "you're losing me. Let me get this right: you saw them together, Trent and Wormsley, and soon after that she left the course?"

"That's right."

"And this boyfriend came onto the scene ..."

"It was more or less the same time. I saw him at the college, waiting for her, I think, and it was around then, and no more than a couple of weeks later – I don't remember seeing her, in fact I never saw her again."

"And did you think there was any relation – I mean, between you catching them together and her leaving?"

"I did wonder. But I'd have thought it would have been Wormsley who would have left, if it came out, if there was a complaint." She stopped talking and eyed the detective closely, as though seeing him for the first time. "Wait a minute ... you don't think ..?"

She clasped a hand across her mouth as though to stifle a yell. "You think he might have killed her?"

"We are making enquiries," said Mills, "not leaping to any conclusions. Earlier you mentioned rumours?"

"There was a lot of gossip doing the rounds, all sorts of stuff; that her boyfriend had thumped Wormsley - that was a favourite. Wormsley took some time off around then, there was a temporary stand in for two or three weeks as I recall, and I suppose that fuelled the rumour mill. You know how it is, particularly with so many teenagers with too much time on their hands and a lot of imagination and hormones working overtime."

Mills didn't, but he nodded all the same. "And Wormsley eventually returned to the college?"

"He did, and by that time Stacey had left, if I'm remembering it right. But I'm almost certain." She had a distant look on her face, like she was recalling something. "I also remember that Wormsley was a bit more restrained after that. Some were saying he must have learned a lesson. I thought maybe he'd had a warning, from the college, or perhaps from Stacey's boyfriend, because he was definitely what I would call subdued when he first came back. But I don't think it lasted. I think he kept his reputation more or less intact most of the time that I was there."

Mills crept back out of the house, feeling as though he had engaged in an illicit affair. He looked up at the front bedroom curtains as he got into his car, half expecting to see them twitch and an angry face bearing down on him.

CHAPTER TWENTY SEVEN

The detectives compared notes. Mills said, "Val Hackett is off the suspect list?"

"We're still keeping an eye on her," said Tyler. "The wedding anniversary has just passed, but her late-husband's birthday is coming up. Better safe than sorry, wouldn't you agree?"

"I didn't think Carstairs went in for surveillance operations."

"It will be limited; low key and just for that day. And we can scratch another one off the list while we're at it. They've been having problems again with the slapper – that's Stan Baker to you. They got an address and I paid a visit. He's eighty odd going on ninety, and a miracle of modern science, and more to the point he has broken the mould by having an alibi for Sunday night."

"Where was he?"

"Around at his daughter's house. She lives in the next street."

"The punters really do get to stay in with family on Sunday evenings," said Mills. "Does she know about his ..."

"Predilections?"

"Something like that."

"I think she had her suspicions about him visiting *The Sweet Box*. She said he'd always been a bit 'high octane' as she described it. Said his late wife had remarked to her daughter that she never knew where he got his energy from. And I had a word with him about slapping the girls. He insisted they liked it and I assured him they didn't. But it wouldn't require the services of a psychiatrist to conclude that there's a bit of senile dementia creeping in, so I don't expect my warning to be heeded for long. So we're down to just the Two Amigos, now. But Hately's firing on all cylinders, apparently, going round to *West End Girls* two, even three times a day asking for his beloved Scarlet."

"To be young and in love," said Mills.

"Meanwhile, back in the real world: your thoughts on Wormsley?"

"There's something there, sir, no doubt about it. It seems likely Trent had a relationship with Wormsley while she was at the college in Shelton, and left her studies soon afterwards."

"He sent her off the rails and into the hands of the mysterious Kev?" said Tyler.

"But why did she turn up in his class two years later, at a different college ... unless of course she was threatening him?"

Tyler recalled what May Lillistock had said to him at *The Sweet Box*. Kelly having a thing with Stacey and the two of them trying to get money out of a teacher Stacey reckoned had 'cradle-snatched' her at college.

"Is Lillistock suggesting blackmail?" asked Mills. "But why leave it that long? Maybe someone else gave Trent the idea."

"Do you have somebody in mind?"

"It could be almost anyone: her boyfriend - or ex - Stewart; Rayworth, Kelly. They seem to come as a package. Maybe they worked as a syndicate."

Tyler nodded and a smile lit up into a dark grin. "You have been putting in the overtime, or at least your imagination has. I've a feeling to invite them all down here, what do you think?"

"I think that's an idea," said Mills.

"I was thinking along the lines of a party."

"I like a party, sir."

"Before we start sending out the invites I want to try something first. Let's see what happens when we turn up the heat in the psychology department, shall we?"

*

Wormsley was in the interview room and maintaining his cool until Mills confronted him with the blackmail scenario.

"You were seen with her, with Stacey Trent, by at least one other student. Do you deny that?" The sweat was beginning to pool beneath the man's fringe, glistening under the lights. "She left the course soon afterwards, but more recently turned up at your Monday evening class, at a different college. Why would she do that?"

"I've really no idea."

"She was threatening you, wasn't she? Blackmailing you?"

"Don't be ridiculous," said Wormsley. But the conviction was lacking. Mills watched him, while Tyler waited in the wings. Nervous movements betraying him; something about to come out, but needing a little more coaxing.

At last Tyler said, "As things stand, you have a credible motive for murdering Stacey Trent. She came back to cause trouble and you chose to shut her up for good."

The hands went up, and their owner appeared grateful for the opportunity to move decisively and to let out some of the energy that was evidently building up inside. "Okay, so I admit that I had a brief fling," said Wormsley, wiping the sweat from his face as he

144

spoke. "She led me on and I should have resisted. We stole a classroom kiss and I realised I was being foolish, and so I pulled back and that was it."

"I see," said Tyler. "And you think we fell out of a Christmas tree?"

"It was more than my job was worth. Why would I risk my reputation, my career, everything that I had worked for, on some cheap tart?"

"You wouldn't be the first, or no doubt the last, Mr Wormsley."

"She turned up in my class and I knew straight away that it meant trouble. But I'm not in a position to turn students away. When students enrol it is my duty to offer my services, and to teach them."

Tyler's eyes widened a fraction at the phrase 'offer my services' but otherwise the DCI retained a neutral expression. "What kind of trouble did you envisage?"

"Well, isn't it obvious?"

"So it was blackmail."

"Alright, she tried it on. She approached me, after class, and said she wanted money or else she'd ruin me. She was trying her luck."

"And you did what, exactly?"

"I told her to go to hell."

"And ..?"

"She said she was going nowhere. That she would keep turning up until I agreed to her terms."

"And then she stopped turning up," said Tyler. "The problem conveniently went away. You saw to that, isn't that right, Mr Wormsley?"

"I didn't kill her. I didn't even threaten her."

"Okay," said Tyler. "Let's paint a picture, shall we? You, as you so memorably described it, *stole a classroom kiss* – which you also described as a *fling* –

145

and yet this young woman then goes to the trouble of enrolling for one of your classes, turning up week after week, in the hope that you will pay her off. Was the extent of your *fling* really nothing more than *a classroom kiss*?"

"More or less, yes."

"Define more or less for me."

"It happened a couple of times."

"Mr Wormsley, please," said Tyler.

"Okay, I went to her house."

"Ah," said Tyler. "Possibly more than a classroom kiss, then."

"I offered to run her home one afternoon. She was living with her parents, a rather grand place it was too. She told me her parents were away for a few days and she invited me in. I shouldn't have accepted, I realise that, of course I do. It was a stupid mistake."

"Yet one that you repeated?"

"They ... were away for a month."

"I see," said Tyler. "And while the cat's away ..."

"I knew it was wrong."

"But that beautiful big house and that beautiful young student ..."

"I saw her for a couple of weeks, possibly three weeks."

"And who ended the affair?"

"I did."

"And how did she take it?"

"She was upset."

"Did she threaten to report you?"

"No, she didn't."

"Did she continue to attend your classes?"

He shook his head. "She stopped attending my classes."

Tyler said, "And do you consider yourself responsible for derailing her studies?"

Wormsley appeared to be scratching around for something to say, but in the end his head dropped. "I suppose I do," he said at last. "I didn't give it a lot of thought at the time. She was still around the college for a short while after that, not in my classes, but around the campus, and I saw her in the company of a young man and assumed she had a boyfriend and had moved on. At some point I stopped seeing her around. But students drop out for all sorts of reasons, and at the time I didn't give it any thought, like I said."

"And the next time that you saw her was when she turned up at your Monday evening class in Fenton?"

"That's right."

The detectives headed up to the CID office. "I can't make my mind up about him," said Tyler. "He's either the coolest customer I've come across in a long time, or else he's telling it straight."

"I think there's more that he's not telling us," said Mills.

"I'm inclined to agree. I intend to let him sweat for a little while, and then we are going to pay him a visit. Not living in splendour, I hear?"

"Not exactly. That house has seen better times, and yet he must be on a decent wage."

"I wonder where his money goes," said Tyler, "or where it went. He must have had Trent down as a little rich girl, having spent the best part of a month round at her parents' palace."

"Ironic," said Mills.

"What is?"

"Her parents believing it was this Kev who derailed her career, when all the time it was a man of apparent

147

respectability and good standing who was doing the damage."

"That all remains conjecture at this stage, of course," said Tyler.

His phone was ringing. He took the call, all the time his eyes fixed on Mills. At last he placed the receiver down, slowly. "That anniversary," he said.

"What about it?"

"Val Hackett. We were keeping an eye open for the weekend. It would have been her late husband's sixty fifth birthday."

"That's right, sir. What is it?"

"It looks like we overlooked a more pressing anniversary. Last night marked forty years since they opened *The Sweet Box*."

"What's happened?" asked Mills, moving forward in his seat.

"Get your coat," he said. "I'll tell you in the car."

CHAPTER TWENTY EIGHT

The fire engines had taken over a section of Waterloo Road, and while smoke continued to rise from the embers of what remained of the building, the fire had now been contained.

The emergency call had come just after dawn, and the fire had quickly taken hold. The call had come from a passer-by, and the early summons and prompt arrival of the emergency services prevented the fire spreading to the adjoining properties.

"There was no-one found in the building?" Tyler asked the chief fire officer as they stood outside the smoking ruins. The officer confirmed that was the case. But it didn't require an expert to confirm that the days of *The Sweet Box* were well and truly over.

The passer-by who reported the fire hadn't seen anyone around, and no-one had as yet come forward to report suspicious activity in the immediate vicinity prior to the blaze. The fire appeared to have started at the rear of the property. A small courtyard accessed by an unsecured iron gate would have provided cover to anyone entering and, presumably, setting fire to the locked, bolted and chained, and generally unused, wooden back door.

Tyler and Mills drove to the home of Val Hackett. They found the property empty. Eric Faron, on the other hand, was at home in his flat. The detectives hammered at his door, and at last Faron appeared, looking dishevelled and somewhat bewildered, giving the impression that he had, as he claimed, indeed been fast asleep in his bed.

"What have I done?" he asked.

"You tell me," said Tyler.

Faron claimed to have been in his flat all evening and in bed since midnight.

"Val Hackett?" said Tyler.

"She used to run the sweet shop," said Faron.

"Doing her a favour, were you?"

"I don't know what you're talking about."

"Forty years since the sweet shop opened, forty years to the day."

"They should never have turned it into a place like that."

"She asked you to do it, didn't she – or did you take it upon yourself?"

Faron looked blank. "What am I supposed to have done?"

Mills took a call on his radio. "Sir," he said.

The detectives stepped outside the flat. "What is it?" snapped Tyler.

"Hackett has just handed herself in at the station."

*

She was in the custody suite, looking defiant. They awaited the arrival of the duty solicitor before beginning the interview.

Hackett sat calmly, her eyes never moving off DCI Tyler while he questioned her. She claimed to have used petrol to start the fire. She also claimed to have worked entirely alone. "I did it for Phil," she said. "And I don't care what you do to me now."

"Attempted murder," said Tyler, "is a very serious charge."

"I didn't try to kill anyone, I already told you that."

"You didn't know that the building was unoccupied. How could you have known?"

150

The first sign of doubt appeared in her eyes, but was quickly vanquished. "There was nobody there. I know what time they leave. I know their comings and goings. I've been watching them a long time."

"Was Eric Faron also watching for you?" asked Tyler.

"I know Eric. He was a regular customer of mine. But he had nothing to do with this. I did it, me, alone, for Phil. And that's all there is to it. You weren't interested in stopping that filthy business - that insult to the memory of my Phil. So I took the law into my own hands. You left me no other choice. I put paid to that place, but I never intended to hurt anyone, let alone kill them."

Her look of defiance was, thought Mills, almost a thing of beauty.

"Do what you like," she said, "lock the door and throw away the key for all I care."

CHAPTER TWENTY NINE

Carstairs was waiting. "DCI Tyler, my office, now."

Old ghosts rising; a schoolboy, an orphan, at the mercy of men in dark uniforms, handing out sadistic retributions for trivial offences, and no-one to speak for the young Jim Tyler, not a soul willing to stand up for him. And now summoned once again by a figure in authority dressed darkly, suitably stern and looking for blood.

A complaint of repeated harassment submitted by Eric Faron, and a reasonable one at that in the eyes of Chief Superintendant Carstairs. And repeated threats from Hackett to burn down *The Sweet Box* failing to result in any action being taken. The beauty of hindsight, of course, but still: how clear did she have to make it that she had something planned? Lack of research from a senior detective: research that might have established the significance of an anniversary that had now been marked in fire. And still no charge brought against her, or against anyone else, for the murder of Stacey Trent.

Tyler's report was on the desk and Carstairs tapped the front of it. "Not very impressive, is it?"

Tyler gave no response. But Carstairs wasn't finished with the question.

"I said, DCI Tyler -"

"It is what it is." Tyler stood up. "If there's nothing else, I have work to be getting on with."

He left the room and walked into the CID office.

Mills looked up as the DCI took his seat.

"Remember that party that I talked to you about? I'd say that now is as good a time as any."

Mills nodded and started making the calls, while Tyler went out into the fresh air.

*

It was a couple of hours later when he returned to the station, and Mills could see right off that something had changed. There was an old look about him, an uncompromising conviction that heralded ominous forebodings. From bitter experience, Mills knew that neither hell nor high water could stand in the way of Jim Tyler when he wore that look.

"How did you get on?"

"The party is on," said Mills.

"Good work."

"Carstairs was looking for you earlier."

"What a damned shame," said Tyler. "He must have just missed me."

Mills offered a look of concern. "Everything alright, Jim?"

"As a matter of fact, no, it isn't. But it will be."

Mills waited, and at last Tyler let out a sigh. "I'm thinking of calling it a day, Danny." The DS started to speak, but Tyler stopped him. "I've already written the letter, and I wouldn't expect Carstairs to try to talk me out of it. The only reason it's not already on his desk, with me sitting at home with my feet up and contemplating the rest of my life out of this game, is that I want one last poke at nailing the case."

He watched Mills scrambling around, trying to work out which question to ask first.

"I owe you an explanation, Danny, and this is the best that I can do. This case has revealed to me a truth I long feared and can no longer deny. I've lost my instinct for the job, and without that I've nothing to offer. I rely too heavily on good fortune. I lead a charmed life." The bitterness saturated the room. "Without the good will and support of you and Graham Berkins, I'd be nowhere. I've been on borrowed time for too long. When you live on the edge, your luck can't hold forever. Inevitably I will become a liability."

He smiled, and Mills couldn't stand it. "I'll tell you the truth," he said. "I've never heard so much self pitying nonsense in all my life!"

"There you go," said Tyler. "I can't even make a decent job of my valedictory speech."

Mills shook his head in disgust. "If you're feeling sorry for yourself, fair enough, we all do that from time to time – but don't you dare lay this at the feet of me and Berkins. Don't come the bloody hero and try to make out that you're really doing us both a big favour, when the truth is you're just having a bad day, with Carstairs on your back and no break in the case."

For a moment Tyler looked shell shocked. Then he regained his composure. "You don't see any merit in the wisdom of jumping before you're pushed?"

"That's not Jim Tyler talking. If you're sick of the job, that's one thing, I couldn't fault you there. But everything else you've said is so much bullshit."

Again Tyler smiled, and then he began to laugh. "You know, Danny, you are right. So, when is the party scheduled to start?"

CHAPTER THIRTY

Rayworth, Stewart, Kelly and Wormsley were placed into separate interview rooms. Carstairs was out attending a meeting, expected back later, and with a memo on Tyler's desk demanding he report to the chief superintendant's office on his return.

Tyler took a coin out of his pocket and tossed it into the air. "Heads," he said. "Observe this new method of policing." He repeated the procedure, Mills looking on un-amused. "Heads again." He tossed the coin for the third time. "Tails."

He pocketed the coin and stood up. "I will not waste valuable time explaining the finer details of this method, but suffice to say that we will make a start with Stewart, progress to Rayworth and Kelly, and then see what Wormsley has to offer by way of a grand finale."

Mills followed the DCI down towards the interview rooms. It wasn't the first time that he had been at a complete loss as to the workings of Tyler's mind. Or the first time he had feared that the great man's judgement was clouded by other agendas setting him on course for destruction. Yet such a thing was faith, and Mills was trying with all his might to hold on to what was left of his.

Stewart was looking at his watch when the detectives entered the interview room. "I start my shift in a couple of hours," he said. "I don't know what else I can tell you about Stacey."

"You know Geoff Wormsley," said Tyler.

"Who is he?" asked Stewart.

The response appeared genuine, but Tyler had been fooled too many times over the years, and remained unconvinced. "You said the last straw with Stacey was when she let you down one Monday evening. But you knew what she was doing on Monday evenings, didn't you?"

"Did I?" said Stewart. Again Tyler studied the young man's face, and it was still hard to read. Were his instincts failing him completely? Was that resignation letter nestling down there in his jacket pocket better placed on the chief superintendent's desk and done with?

"What was Stacey doing on Monday evenings?" Tyler asked Stewart.

"I don't know what she was doing. Seeing someone else I imagine."

"And that didn't bother you? It didn't make you angry? It didn't cause you to follow her, to see where she was going, and who she might be seeing?"

"No, it didn't. I've never been the possessive type. If she wanted to see other men .... it was time for me to move on. I'm sorry what happened to her, obviously I am, who wouldn't be? But it was nothing to do with me."

"She talked to you about going back to college."

"She mentioned it. She mentioned a lot of things."

"She didn't tell you that she had enrolled at a college, and was taking an evening class on Mondays?"

"You're kidding me?"

The surprise appeared genuine, thought Tyler. "Did you ever meet her parents?"

Stewart laughed. "She wasn't that kind of girl."

"Did she ever talk about her parents?"

"Not really. I got the feeling she didn't like them much."

"You never visited their house?"

"No – why would I?"

Tyler asked Stewart to remain in the interview room, while he and Mills moved next door.

Rayworth spoke as they entered. "What's it about now?" she said. "Have you found something?"

Tyler asked her about Wormsley. She didn't appear to know the name. He asked if she knew that Stacey was attending a night class on Monday evenings.

"She said she was thinking of going back to school." But according to Rayworth, she didn't know that Stacey had actually started attending a class. "It's that bastard Kelly you want to be speaking to. He was seeing her, I'd put money on it, but he won't admit it. Makes you wonder what he's got to hide, doesn't it?"

"What do you mean by that?" asked Tyler.

"Well, you can fill in the blanks, I'm sure. He gets rough when he doesn't get his own way. Stacey wasn't the type to stay faithful, went her own way and did her own thing, and Jon doesn't like women with a mind of their own."

"You are suggesting that he killed her?"

"I can't prove anything but I'd say he's capable."

"Let me get this straight," said Tyler. "You accuse Kelly of seeing Trent behind your back ... and now you're saying -"

"You think I'm just being spiteful? That I'm making trouble for him because he did the dirty on me? You don't know the half of it. Because you don't know Kelly, what he's like."

Kelly sat calmly as the detectives joined him in the third interview room. Before Tyler had chance to ask a question, he said, "Has she confessed yet?"

Tyler offered a blank expression. "Mr Kelly?"

"Rayworth – has she fessed up to killing her? She knew I was seeing her, and she couldn't stand it. I was sick of the grief I was getting, and I went with Stacey, and as soon as I heard what happened, well, part of me knew it was Christine that did it. You don't cross her."

"Interesting," said Tyler. "Let's pick the bones out of what you've just told me. You say that you suspected Rayworth of killing Stacey, and yet you didn't think to pass on your suspicions to the police, not even when they conveniently appeared on your doorstep. You also suggest that you were intimidated by Rayworth, and yet you remained with her, even though, if your suspicions were correct, she had killed Stacey after discovering that she was having a relationship with you?"

Kelly didn't answer.

"You can see my confusion?" said Tyler. "What you say makes absolutely no sense to me whatsoever. Perhaps you would like to help me understand what I am clearly struggling with, Mr Kelly."

"I was scared of what she would do."

"That part I can grasp. And yet, knowing how dangerous she can be, you still chose to engage in a relationship with her friend and colleague."

"Stacey ... she could be very persuasive. I was stupid. I shouldn't have done it. But I did, and then I was scared Christine would find out."

Tyler listened intently, and gestured to Kelly to continue.

"Looking back, I reckon Stacey was doing it to hurt Christine. They'd fallen out over something, I don't know what. I think Stacey used me."

"And you didn't think to spill any of this the last time we talked?"

"I didn't think you'd believe me. I thought you might think I had something to do with it. A man scared of a woman – who's going to believe that? But I was scared, and I reckon she did it – Christine did it. She's off her head. And she's trying to fit me up with what she's done."

"Geoff Wormsley," said Tyler.

"Who?"

"Tell me about Geoff Wormsley."

At last, thought Tyler; that flicker in the eye; that betrayal of deceit beyond all doubt. When it was there, it was unmistakable. You couldn't miss it, brief though it might be.

And Kelly had the same instincts; and what he had seen in the eye of the detective was every bit as certain. Tyler wasn't bluffing; because Tyler knew. "I know that name," said Kelly.

"I'm sure that you do," said Tyler. He waited, and all the time he could see Kelly trying to read him, to work out what he already knew.

At last Kelly said, "He was that teacher, wasn't he?"

"*That teacher?*" said Tyler. "What teacher would that be, exactly?"

"She told me about him. One time we were talking, and she said she'd been at college, and that this dirty old bastard was trying it on. That was him, wasn't it?"

"What else did she say?"

Kelly was still weighing it up, trying to judge how much to say; but Tyler had no doubt that Kelly knew.

159

"She said he was why she left college."

"What – she left college because this teacher had 'tried it on'?"

"It was more than that. She had a thing with him, and when that thing was over he told her that it was time she thought about a different course, or a different college. He told her he would make sure she failed."

"Why didn't she report him?"

"She didn't think they would believe her. He told her they'd think it was sour grapes because she was failing, and she would have been, so she was trying to make trouble. In the end she just left."

"Did you know she went back to college, Mr Kelly?"

Kelly looked at Tyler, and then across at Mills. The calmness had returned. He had the manner of someone about to turn over a well kept ace.

"I knew she was planning to. She said she intended to pay him back ... bleed him dry."

CHAPTER THIRTY ONE

Wormsley was chewing at his finger ends when he again received the company of the two detectives. He looked as though he hadn't slept in a week, and he wasted no time in delivering what he called a full confession.

Wormsley admitted to the affair with Trent; and that when she turned up at his new place of work, enrolled onto the Monday night Psychology course that he was delivering, she made it immediately clear what her aims and objectives were on taking up the subject.

"I couldn't believe it when she walked in."

"*Of all the classrooms in all the world*," said Tyler, under his breath, "*she had to walk into mine.*"

"After the class, she came up to me, and said that she wanted a word."

It must have felt like old times, thought Tyler. "What did she say?"

"Not a lot. Just that she intended to take me for every penny I had."

"And did she?"

"She arrived too late for that."

"Meaning?"

"My life was already in a bigger mess than hers." Wormsley laughed, and the sound was hollow and sardonic. "I told her that if she could find any money then she was welcome to it. She didn't believe me, of course she didn't. I had a good job; I'd been doing that job for years. It didn't make sense to her that I could be in debt."

Tyler looked at Mills and the questions passed tacitly between them.

"Not a clamour of other ex students coming back to haunt you?" asked Tyler.

Wormsley shook his head. "Only the one, thank God. I got into gambling. I was even seeing a therapist about my habit. But I couldn't shake it, and I still can't, to tell you the truth."

"And you told her?"

"I kept telling her. And she kept turning up. Then, about two weeks ago, she came to my house."

"She came alone?"

"There was a car parked outside, a man in it. He waited for her. I showed her bank statements, letters from debt companies. She looked around my house and saw that there was nothing of any value left. She told me what she thought of me, what she hadn't already said. I took it. She was right, and I deserved every word. Before she left, she said she'd be keeping an eye on me, to see if my fortunes changed. That's the last time that I saw her."

"And if your fortunes did change, what, she'd be back?" said Tyler.

"Yes."

Tyler waited to hear if anything else was to follow. When it didn't, he said, "And then your fortunes did change, didn't they?"

"What?"

"She was found dead, Mr Wormsley. One less worry for you, I imagine."

"I had nothing to do it - with her death. I've done some stupid things in my time, but I'm not a killer."

"She didn't threaten you with violence?"

"Not directly. But coming to my house ... and the man waiting outside in the car ... I took that to be a warning."

"Would you recognise the man if you saw him again?" asked Tyler.

"I doubt it. He was wearing dark glasses and a cap. He was parked across the road."

The detectives stood out in the corridor. "Time to reprise an old trick," said Tyler.

Mills knew it well enough, remembered it from a few years back. But this time a variation; that old fire alarm ploy.

Tyler positioning himself in the waiting room at the end of the corridor leading off from the interview rooms, the desk sergeant primed to set off the alarm for thirty seconds, Mills waiting out in the corridor. As the bells began ringing, Mills entered the four interview rooms, gathering the occupants to follow him to the nearest fire point, where Tyler stood waiting.

The bells had already stopped. "False alarm," he said, addressing the assembly. "We can all go back to our rooms now, sorry about that." Kelly and Rayworth eyed each other with venom but said nothing. Then Rayworth saw Stewart, who lowered his eyes, Kelly looking over at Stewart now, but not a word spoken by anyone. Tyler was watching Wormsley, his eyes flicking around the gathering, coming back to rest on Kelly. Then Kelly, appearing to sense the eyes on him, caught Wormsley's look.

With the four back in their respective interview rooms, the detectives resumed their discussion with Wormsley. "Anyone there you recognise?" asked Tyler.

"Convenient fire alarm," he said.

"Can't fool a psychologist," said Tyler.

163

"I can't be sure," said Wormsley. "It might have been either of them, or neither of them. I take it they were friends of Stacey?"

The detectives stood together out in the corridor. Tyler said, "That would have been a lucky bonus, but not the object of the exercise. We'll leave Kelly stewing the longest. The way he was looking at Wormsley, that's where my money's going. He's also going to be working overtime on what Rayworth's telling us, and vice versa."

"And Stewart?"

"Still the wild card. Isn't this fun?"

"Carstairs is going to be asking about that fire alarm."

"You are a born worrier, Danny. But would you deny me the opportunity of going out in a blaze of glory?"

"I hope you know what you're doing?"

"Isn't it obvious? I'm shuffling the deck and hoping for a lucky break. I'm sure Wormsley would cringe at the metaphor."

They went in to see Stewart. "See anyone out there you don't know?" said Tyler.

"I don't know that old guy."

Old, thought Mills, instantly feeling the years and fleetingly questioning where they had gone.

Tyler observed, once again, that either Stewart was the most accomplished liar he had ever encountered, or else he'd genuinely never clapped eyes before on Wormsley. He tried the name again, and this time the recognition was there, no question.

"I know that name," said Stewart. He appeared to be trying to gain the context.

"College?" prompted Tyler.

He nodded. "Stacey told me about an old lecturer trying it on. She said that's why she finished college. Was that the creep?"

The detectives stood outside the interview room containing Rayworth. "Was that just too cute?" asked Mills.

"Still tough to call, I'd say," said Tyler.

Rayworth was true to form. "What is that bastard saying?"

"Which 'bastard' are we referring to?" asked Tyler.

"Kelly, who else?"

"You wouldn't say that Stewart had a motive, if his girlfriend had ditched him for your boyfriend?"

"He hasn't the bottle. Dean Stewart is like a wet weekend. I don't know what Stacey ever saw in him."

"Which just leaves you and Kelly, then." Rayworth was glaring, seemingly beyond words. "And if Stacey had gone off with your boyfriend, why would he kill her?"

"Because he's off his head, that's why. You don't know him."

"We need a little bit more than that, I'm afraid. Does the name Geoff Wormsley *ring any bells*?"

"That's the teacher." A look came over her. "That was him, out there?"

"You've seen him before?"

"No, but Stacey told me about him. He looks the type. You saying he did it, to shut her up?" She grinned. "Going back to college – that's what she was up to, the crafty ..."

The detectives stood outside the final door.

"Summarise for me, Danny. I want to know that I'm on the right track."

165

Mills took a few moments, assembling it all in his head. "Rayworth would jump at anything, anyone, if she was guilty. But she didn't."

"I'm not so sure. She's willing to accept that either Kelly or Wormsley is the killer."

"But not Stewart. On balance, I believe she's innocent."

"And what about Wormsley?"

"I'm inclined to believe him, too. I'm still not sure about Stewart."

"He gives good answers," said Tyler.

"Perhaps that's the problem."

"You are notoriously hard to please, do you know that? Anyway, I think Kelly has sweated long enough."

CHAPTER THIRTY TWO

Kelly was trying hard to maintain a facade of cool. It was frayed around the edges and Mills saw a young man ready to crack open and spill what was lurking inside.

"You met Stacey Trent after her shift ended on Sunday night, didn't you?" said Tyler.

"I didn't kill her, I swear it."

"You met her, though. And if you want us to believe that you didn't kill her, then you'd better start telling the truth."

"Okay," he said, his eyes shifting from one detective to the other, looking like the walls were closing in around him. "Fair enough. But I swear -"

"Tell us what happened, Jon."

Kelly told the story, and it came out in a single outpouring and without hesitation. He was seeing Trent even before her relationship with Stewart had ended. And like Stewart, he wondered what she was doing with her Monday evenings.

"He most probably thought she was seeing someone. But it wasn't me, at least not on a Monday. So I got nosy and one time I followed her. She went to that college, the one in Fenton."

Kelly didn't tell her that he had followed her. But one time they were talking together and he asked her what plans she had for the future.

"She got upset. I hadn't seen her like that before. I asked her what was wrong and she told me about the teacher at college assaulting her. She said that she'd thought about going back to study, getting out of the game. She regretted everything, and blamed that piece of garbage for screwing everything up, and that's why she ended up getting in with a loser like Kev Blake, and getting into all kinds of shit."

"You took her round to the teacher's house, didn't you? You waited outside in the car?"

"I didn't go in. I didn't get out of the car."

"Your role being ..?" asked Tyler.

"I drove her. That was it. And I was there in case he tried anything, you know, turned nasty."

"Not to add some intimidation?"

"Is that what he told you? I never even met him. I saw him answer the door, and when Stacey left his house. I never spoke to him, not once."

"You were hoping for your cut, though, isn't that right?"

"No, it's not how it was. I was there to support her. Despite what Christine says about me, I hate men who hurt women, exploit them. When she told me what she was doing Monday evenings, and that she was planning to punish him for what he did, I was all for it, but not because I wanted anything out of it."

"Why did she tell you what she was doing, if she didn't need you to intimidate Wormsley and you weren't after a cut?"

"I think she needed to tell someone. And we got so we could talk, you know, really say what was on our minds, and what we wanted out of life."

Tyler turned the subject back to the night of the murder, and Kelly told the detectives how he arranged to meet her after she finished her shift.

"Where did you plan to meet?"

"At the lido."

"Why there? She lives close by, so why not meet at her flat?"

"She was paranoid about being watched, being followed. She was certain her flat was being watched, or bugged, or something."

"Did she suggest who might be doing that?"

"She thought it might be Christine."

"But she worked with Christine, and left *West End Girls* at the same time that night."

Kelly shrugged. "I don't know. But she wanted to meet me at the lido. And she asked if I would follow her, to make sure that she wasn't being followed by Christine, if you see what I mean."

"*The irony just keeps piling up,*" muttered Tyler.

"So, I followed her to the lido, and I was fairly sure no-one was following me."

"And then what?"

Suddenly Kelly appeared coy.

"What is it?"

"Well, it's like – Stacey liked doing weird things sometimes. I think she enjoyed danger. She wanted to have sex behind the hut on the lido. I told her someone might pass by, but she said I was chicken. She said it made it more exciting. You never knew what to expect when you were with her. I liked that. So, anyway, we did it, you know. And ..."

"Yes?" said Tyler.

"It was strange."

"What was?"

"I felt like I was being watched. I had this feeling, and I couldn't shake it. She kept asking me what was wrong. But it was like we really were being watched. There was someone around."

"You didn't see anyone?"

"No, I didn't actually see anyone."

Tyler said, "Who do you think was watching you?"

"Can't you guess?" said Kelly. "I reckon she doubled back and followed us. She says she got back to the flat first, but she's lying about that. It was me that got there first."

"And you believe Rayworth killed Stacey after you left?"

"I think she might have done, yes."

Mills struck up. "Why did Stacey remain at the lido, and not go home when you left?"

Kelly shrugged again. "Why did she do anything?"

"You didn't think that was suspicious?" said Mills.

"Not really, no. She said she was staying for a bit, it was a nice warm evening. Stacey always did her own thing, *always*."

"It must have been getting late."

Tyler and Kelly both looked at the DS. Mills took the point. His grandmother had always instilled in him that an hour in bed before midnight was worth two hours afterwards, and he'd always tried to live by that, except of course when he had been working nights.

Tyler resumed his own questioning. "What about Stewart?" he said. "Could it have been her old boyfriend, checking up on her?"

"I suppose it could have been."

"But you'd prefer to think that it was Rayworth?"

"What's that supposed to mean?"

"You say that she lied about being back at the flat first. That suggests she was bent on implicating you. I wonder if you aren't therefore trying to make a case against her."

"Why would she lie about being back first, unless she had something to hide?"

170

Tyler stood up and Mills followed him out into the corridor, and then back into the interview room where Rayworth sat waiting. He asked her again about that evening, and again she insisted that she had gone straight back to the flat after her shift ended, and that Kelly had come in later.

"And you think he was seeing her?"

"It makes sense. They were as bad as each other."

"Why would he kill her?"

"I don't know. Maybe she was threatening to tell me what the bastard was up to. Maybe she told him to sling his hook and he couldn't take it. With an ego as big as that, you don't take rejection easily."

"What about Stewart?"

"What about him?"

"If he saw them together, who knows how he might have taken it?"

"Anything's possible. Some people can keep their anger, their jealousy, better hidden than others."

"You'd put Stewart in that bracket?"

"I don't know. But I'd say it was one of them, because it certainly wasn't me."

"Not even for stealing your man?" asked Tyler.

"*Man*? That's a laugh! She was welcome to him."

The four suspects went on their ways, at staggered intervals, and Tyler and Mills retired to the CID office. There was a message from Carstairs waiting for Tyler: he was to report to the chief's office first thing in the morning.

"He probably wants to know who forgot to change the batteries in the fire alarm."

"And why we still haven't charged anyone for Trent's murder," suggested Mills.

"We could go around in circles until old age gets the better of us. But I'm still not convinced any of that lot did it. Rayworth's added Stewart to her list of possibilities but it doesn't fit somehow, none of it does. Don't get me wrong, I trust them about as much as a cartel of chief superintendents ..."

He looked at Mills. "Go on, then, feel free to disagree with me."

CHAPTER THIRTY THREE

Once the kids were in bed Mills settled down in front of the TV with his wife. The local news was coming on the BBC.

Mills looked on in disbelief. A reporter was standing outside the ruins of *The Sweet Box*, interviewing a small group of mostly women. The gathering held up banners with a photograph of Val Hackett, the word **HERO** above the picture in bold lettering.

According to the women interviewed, Hackett had done what the authorities in the city had failed to do: they had closed down a business that brought nothing but trouble to the area, attracting predatory men, making the neighbourhood even more unsafe than it already was.

The women suggested that, far from brothels making the sex trade safer for the workers, the recent murder of an employee at *The Sweet Box* showed that to be a complete fallacy. The brothels were all about money, and legitimising the trade was doing nothing to keep women safe in the city. It had taken a murder and a fire for the authorities to wake up to the problem, and now it was time to do something about it. They could start by closing down the 'sister' business owned by the same woman, Hayley Greener.

Cut to footage of *West End Girls*.

Then Carstairs appeared, with what looked like Cedar Lane Police Station posing in the background. He wasn't saying much, and using a lot of words in the process. Mills had little doubt that he would go far in the department.

Carstairs managed to say that every effort was being made to bring the killer of Stacey Trent to justice, and that arson was a serious crime. The press were plying him ten to the dozen with questions, but they were clearly not getting anything else out of him.

Mills let out a breath. "Bloody hell," he said. "Arsonist turns hero!"

"Looks like you're having fun," said his wife.

"You can't beat it."

"Are you any closer to finding the killer?" she asked him.

"Good question. The killer might well be right under our noses, or else we're grasping at straws. Tyler's in for a hell of a morning."

"Why's that?"

"If they're dragging Carstairs in front of the camera, he's going to be demanding a result and fast. That means more pressure; and Jim's about ready to hand in his notice as it stands."

"You think he will?"

"You never know what he's going to do. He'd love nothing better than to nail this case and present it, tied up in a bow, to Berkins on his return."

"Berkins is coming back?"

"We don't know. But we live in hope. Carstairs doesn't bother me so much, there's a thousand like him out there, and one's as bad as another. But Jim can't stand the sight of him."

"What's new? He doesn't like anyone in authority."

"Can't argue with that," said Mills. "But Berkins knows how to play him, how to bring out the best in him. He trusts Berkins; he doesn't trust Carstairs, and who can blame him. The man's a careerist, and he'll get to the top on the backs of those beneath him if he has to."

"Sounds like you've been talking to Jim Tyler."

"It's true," said Mills. "It's the way it works, in this business and no doubt every other organisation you can think of. I don't like it any more than he does, it's just that I've come to accept it – and he can't. And I admire that. I don't want him to throw in the towel, I want him to stay and fight. He's the best I've known, in spite of his demons."

His wife placed a hand on his. "Nice speech," she said.

"I mean every word."

"I know, and good for you."

They went up to bed. Mills was getting undressed when his wife said, "What's that you're trying to hide from me?"

He looked back at her over his shoulder. "It's no secret," he said. "It's what you signed up for."

She laughed. "I don't mean that! Have you been at the pies again?"

"What kind of a question is that to ask a man about to perform the marital function?"

"I want you to be performing 'the marital function', as you so charmingly put it, for many years to come."

"This case," he said, "it's playing havoc with my diet."

"I can see that."

"Which is why I need the exercise. Doctor's orders, remember?"

He climbed into bed.

"I thought you were going to ask Jim if you could go jogging with him."

"He's really not my type," he said, sidling up to his wife.

"I'm not sure I like the idea of being your exercise machine. It's hardly flattering."

"We all must make sacrifices at some stage," he said. "So, what's it to be, treadmill or trampoline?"

"Are you going to ask him about going out for a run?"

Mills sighed with frustration. "Okay, I promise. If he hands in his letter of resignation, he'll have plenty of time on his hands." She started to ask another question, and Mills raised a hand. "I have to be up in a few hours!"

"You old romantic you."

While Mills was working up a sweat in the confines of his bedroom, Tyler was pounding the streets of the city, winding his way back up towards the doomsday village of Penkhull, where he had lately made his home. But taking the facts of the case out for a late evening run had failed to clarify a thing. The names and faces bounced around in his brain, merging into a quagmire of speculation that left him no further forward in the case. He walked back along Penkhull Terrace, looked to the east, to the sprawl of lights and the darkness of the countryside beyond, and wondered if he would still make this place his home once he had told Carstairs where to stick the job.

Beneath a scalding shower images of past lives and loves flicked through his mind: his failed marriage and the string of brief love affairs that had peppered his time here in this land of exile. How many good women did it take? Was the key to happiness to be found only once the ties to this lonely and brutal occupation were cut for good? Or would he find himself just as lonely but with even more time on his hands with which to fight the monsters that still held sway somewhere deep down in his psyche? Was the job keeping him sane, or preventing him from attaining sanity? It was difficult to tell.

One thing he did know: he owed it to Mills and Berkins not to rise to the provocation of the likes of men like Carstairs. Yet plans had a habit of unravelling, and sometimes in the blink of an eye. He could go to bed with one intention fixed in mind, and the hours of darkness could weave their magic and he would awake with another plan entirely. But still, Mills and Berkins deserved more than weak-willed indulgence. In his time in Staffordshire he hadn't taken a drink, and neither had he felled a senior officer with a well aimed punch, much as both temptations had at times felt near-impossible to deny.

Tyler went to bed, and he dreamed of tyrants and devils, and some he kicked to death on the ground while the sadists that had tormented him as a child had their eyes gouged out and fed to the birds.

He put in a shift and woke up feeling like death.

CHAPTER THIRTY FOUR

Mills had left home with a spring back in his step, and a fresh determination to stick to his new dietary regime, or what his wife insisted on referring to as his lifestyle change. Driving through the countryside, back towards the city, he noticed a board outside the newsagents in Bucknall: **Val Hackett for Mayor!**

Mills parked outside and went in to purchase a copy of The Sentinel, the local newspaper heralding the claim. He quickly found the article and read through it.

There had been a lot of criticism of late regarding Ashley Parker, the current mayor. His lack of action when it came to issues close to the heart of many of the residents of North Staffordshire had created a wave of activity focused on getting him out. And one of the issues he had seemingly stalled on was the plethora of massage parlours that had been springing up around the city. It had become a sensitive issue, and now events on Waterloo Road had given the activists a figurehead, a victim; *a hero*.

"Val Hackett, take a bow!" Mills placed the paper onto the passenger seat and continued his journey to Cedar Lane.

There was no sign of Tyler when he arrived, and Carstairs was already on the prowl. There was a showdown in the air, he could feel it. He was working through the statements given by Kelly, Stewart, Rayworth and Wormsley, but his mind kept slipping away, wondering what was keeping Tyler, his left hand instinctively reaching time and again for the biscuit drawer, to be reminded repeatedly that the immediate environment had been cleared of all temptation.

Carstairs had already been through three times, peering over at the DCI's empty desk. Mills couldn't stand it. He rang Tyler's home phone, hoping it would keep ringing and that his colleague would come bursting through the door with a good excuse for his tardiness.

Tyler picked up.

"Jim, you know what time it is?"

"There's one hell of a campaign brewing to close down *West End Girls*," he said. "And *Val Hackett for mayor* – what do you think about that?"

"Carstairs is like a cat on hot bricks," said Mills.

"Let him stew."

The thought crossed his mind and he voiced it. "You're not ..?"

"What?"

"Calling it a day?"

"What gave you that impression? I'll be in presently. I've a call to make first. Tell you about it later."

The phone clicked down. Mills looked up to see Carstairs approaching. "Heard anything from DCI Tyler yet this morning?"

"No, sir. I expect he will be in soon though."

Carstairs eyed the DS with unveiled suspicion. Then he turned and exited the office, allowing Mills to finally sit back, close his eyes, and smack the desk so hard that his hand was throbbing. *What the bloody hell was Tyler playing at?*

*

The idea had struck him in the early hours, fresh out of nightmares, the notion staring him in the face. May

Lillistock, the dark haired woman he had met at *The Sweet Box.*

Tyler checked the list of contacts and called her. He could hear the sleep in her voice when she answered, but coming awake quickly. Could he call round to see her? When, now? Give me an hour.

Tyler, a man of his word, arrived outside the flat exactly one hour later. Lillistock was dressed in jeans and a long blue shirt, and she looked a different person to the one he had met briefly at *The Sweet Box.* Now the makeup was discreet and tasteful, not vulgar and garish; and the scorching smile that he had previously encountered had mellowed to a modest expression of welcome.

"Coffee?" she asked.

"Thank you," said Tyler. He sat in the uncluttered, tidy living room, in one of the Ikea rocker chairs adjacent to a small occasional table.

She brought the drinks through, placed them both on the table, and then swung a chair around so that it was facing Tyler.

"I understand you're calling it a day," he said.

"Hayley tell you that?"

"She mentioned a deepening staffing crisis, and I put two and two together."

"You detective you," she said, grinning as she sipped at her coffee.

The woman was smart, attractive, hadn't the wasted desperation about her that marked off so many of the women he had spoken to at Greener's establishments. "How did you get into this line of work?" he asked.

"Now that's a question," she said. "How long have we got?"

"I'll come back to it," he said, and she laughed. "You're based at West End now, I take it?"

"I've given them notice to get staff and then I'm on my way."

"Any particular reason you're choosing now to leave?"

She made a play of drumming on her lips, feigning a look of deep concentration. "Oh, now, let me see, what could it be? A colleague is savagely murdered, and then my place of work is burnt to the ground. You're supposed to be the detective, but you might say there's a wakeup call hidden in there."

"You were talking about the affairs of Jon Kelly when Greener interrupted. You said he was your boyfriend before Rayworth -"

"*Moved in on him.* I'm ashamed to say, yes, that's right. So, go on, be a charmer and ask: *what's a sweetie like me doing with a waster like him?*"

"The thought might have occurred," said Tyler, picking up his drink.

"Jon Kelly," she said, "doesn't look much, I'll grant you. But ... he has a way. He's a two-timing, three or four-timing dirt bag from rough stock with few saving graces, but he's good with women. He's the sort we sometimes fall for, knowing we shouldn't. But there it is."

"And he was seeing Rayworth."

"Amongst many others I don't doubt."

"Including Stacey Trent."

"Stacey was a bit like Jon, she couldn't help herself, couldn't get enough of it."

"Did you know much about her?"

"I knew what I knew from the grapevine. It's well active in this line of work I can tell you. Like I said, I

181

keep my ear to the ground. I knew she had rich parents she never saw and couldn't stand. If there was a sniff of money in the air, Jon Kelly's nostrils would be twitching, so it wouldn't surprise me if he was onto her."

"Was – is - Kelly pimping?"

She put her cup down and clapped her hands. "Bravo, detective!"

"That's how you got into the work – through Kelly?"

"That's it, mystery solved."

"Forgive my ignorance," said Tyler, "but why -"

"Why was I working for Greener? It was safer off the streets, and Kelly had an arrangement with her."

"Supplying women to work at *The Sweet Box* and West End?"

"Correctamundo! I sometimes wonder just how many of Greener's angels are Kelly's ex-girlfriends. He might even have the set."

"I don't doubt he has other business interests," said Tyler, eyeing her over the rim of his coffee cup.

"Is that a direct question, or are you just thinking aloud?"

"Is he supplying drugs?"

"I wouldn't know about that," she said, taking a sip from her drink, and still looking straight at Tyler.

"Is that part of the attraction? He keeps his girls in affordable dope and they repay the favours any way they can?"

"You have a dim view of this profession," she said.

"And careless talk can prove dangerous?"

"Are you suggesting that I'm at risk, or that Stacey put herself out there?"

"You tell me."

"Okay. Maybe you're on the right track. But you didn't get any of this from me. I was doing my share of what you call 'dope' when I was with Jon, and then I cleaned my act up. I decided there was more to life, and I could feel the time starting to slip away. Drugs have a habit of making you believe you're going to live forever. Funny how Jon didn't look quite such a catch once I was clean. And I think the feeling was mutual. Desperation and dope are one hell of a combination, and can make even the likes of me compliant."

Tyler thought for a minute. There was no evidence of substance use regarding Stacey Trent.

"Would that same principle apply in the case of Stacey, would you say?"

Lillistock laughed. "Nice try. But is anything ever that simple?"

Tyler finished his drink. "So, what are you saying?"

"Stacey was a rebel, and I mean a genuine, twenty four carat. If all the other girls were doing stuff, then she wouldn't go near it. If that was the deal, then she didn't want to know. She didn't need the money, she didn't need Jon Kelly, or any of his wares, and I think that made her a challenge to Jon. Oh, she was pretty, she didn't need to sell herself in any sense; there would always be buyers for girls like Stacey. But I believe it was all a game to her, and so for someone like Kelly, she was something new, off the scale."

"Do you know Dean Stewart?"

"I don't recognise the name."

He asked where she was on Sunday night. "I wasn't working. I was here most of the evening."

"Here on your own?"

Her smile was warm and knowing. "Still looking for suspects? I was alone, yes – sad, isn't it? I've spent God

183

knows how long pandering to the cheap desires of men, clients as well as the likes of Jon Kelly, and I can't seem to find anyone to hang on to. But in answer to your next question, no, I didn't kill Stacey. Why would I? I hardly knew her. Oh – you mean because she went with Kelly? So did Christine, and no-one's cut her face off – though don't think I haven't considered it."

She placed the empty cup down. "And before you get any ideas, I'm joking." She asked Tyler if he wanted more coffee, and then she made two fresh cups and brought them back through.

"So," she said, "what's your visit here this morning really about?"

CHAPTER THIRTY FIVE

Tyler sat in front of Carstairs.

"*What the hell is going on?*"

As warning shots went, Tyler had to admit it was right up there. It might even have been a formal declaration of war.

Carstairs had the tone, the look, the carefully cultivated no-nonsense attitude, in short all the qualities required of senior management in a modern organisation. The words were delivered apparently in anger and frustration, but Tyler knew that they were far more contrived and calculated than that.

"Can you be more specific?" he asked.

"Let's begin with yesterday's farce, shall we?"

"Farce?" asked Tyler. "That sounds intriguing."

But Carstairs wasn't rising to the bait. "Little wonder we have a chief superintendent off with ulcers." The comment was made under the breath, meant to be heard, and at the same time not a clearly directed accusation.

Tyler smiled at the cheapness of the tactic. He had learned too much to be drawn, but still he couldn't resist a little play. "How is Graham doing?" he asked.

"I'm referring to that *farce* with the fire alarms, after you'd filled up the interview rooms," said Carstairs.

"I wished to observe dynamics, amongst our guests."

"Did you? And are you aware that a fight broke out last night between two of the people you were interviewing?"

Tyler could hazard a guess. "Rayworth and Kelly by any chance?"

Carstairs pulled out the report that Tyler had left him and smacked the front of it with the back of his hand. "I hope for your sake that you're a damned sight further forward."

"Kelly was pimping a good proportion of the work force at both brothels; something of a monopoly, in fact; he likely intimidated Wormsley, who's still too frightened to admit it. I'm guessing that Rayworth attacked Kelly because she suspects he's trying to frame her for murder."

"Why haven't you charged Kelly?"

"What for, being beaten up by his girlfriend - sorry, I mean ex girlfriend?"

"I'm talking about the murder of a young woman, DCI Tyler."

"Because I'm not convinced he's the killer. And we have no evidence to say otherwise. It's just as likely that Rayworth was responsible, and we don't have anything to prove that theory either."

"His story: meeting Trent at the lido, having sex with her out there when she had a flat around the corner - it's laughable!"

"That's why I believe it," said Tyler. "It's the worst cover story for a murder I've ever heard. Kelly isn't stupid enough to make something up like that."

"You're making a lot of assumptions."

"That's true. But then I have little else to go on."

"So what about Val Hackett?"

"What about her?"

Carstairs' fingers were tapping at the report on his desk, his body rigid. "I'll spell it out, shall I? A woman admitting to setting fire to *The Sweet Box*, without any regard whatsoever for human life ..."

They were getting nowhere, and Carstairs' desperation was wearing thin. Pressure on seniority always did, because the senior ranks never failed to pass it on down the chain. Tyler wondered how many times that pressure had resulted in false prosecutions, and in miscarriages of justice. Any result better than no result at all, because the statistics must prevail. But the resistance to that pressure, he had learned the hard way, was every bit as much a part of the job as uncovering evidence to find the real culprits. Hackett had to be punished for what she had done, that was a given; though a host of complex factors had to be fed into the equation if the final result was ever going to look and feel like justice.

But that was for others, more learned and better paid, to decide on.

And the same might be said of Kelly. He might yet need to be taken off the streets, and possibly for a host of reasons, though not for murder, as far as Tyler could tell.

Carstairs was demanding an updated report. As things stood, Tyler was still on the case. The resignation letter was becoming the equivalent of a string of worry beads in his pocket, something to run his fingers over when he needed reassurance – reassurance that this didn't have to go on forever, that there was always a way out and a different way of living. Yet for now his mission in life, the one he was choosing to accept was not to run scared, but to stay and fight, regardless of the consequences. He would find and nail the killer of Stacey Trent, and it would be his gift to the returning Chief Superintendent Berkins, God willing.

*

Tyler returned to the CID office. "Did you get in touch with Trent's parents?" he asked Mills.

"They can see us later. What's this about?"

He told Mills about his visit to Lillistock, and what had been revealed during that second cup of coffee.

Mills thought over what the DCI had told him. "Why didn't she say anything before?"

Tyler told him of his earlier encounter with Lillistock, on a visit to *The Sweet Box*. "You get the feeling sometimes that a person is itching to tell you something. But then they don't. And hours, or even days later, it comes back to you, a missed opportunity, a thing left unspoken. It's that hunch thing again, Danny. I've learned never to disregard it."

"Have you told Carstairs about this?"

"Not yet. I want to talk to the Trents first. I hear Rayworth had another go at Kelly."

"Much damage done?"

"Superficial bruising, a cut lip and a black eye."

"Shame," said Mills. "There's a man who could use a good kicking."

"I can't disagree with you there."

"But you still don't think he's our man?"

"If you mean, did he kill Trent ... I've been known to be wrong before, in fact many times. Anyway, if there's any tea left in this office, I have a report to update. I'm on my very best behaviour from here on in."

"Sir?" said Mills, already at the kettle.

"Why, haven't you heard the news?"

"What news?"

"Berkins is out of hospital. I'm hoping the days of the present regime are numbered."

CHAPTER THIRTY SIX

Jane Trent answered the door. Mills wondered if the grief had passed, the woman appearing lighter in step and in general demeanour than she had done on their previous visit; like a great burden had been lifted.

As though remembering what the detectives' involvement in their lives was, her expression suddenly shifted into one of sorrowful concern. "Have you found who did this?" she asked.

"Our investigation is still ongoing, I'm afraid," said Tyler.

"Oh, I see. It's just, with you wanting to see us, in person. I wondered ..." She invited them through to the spacious sitting room where Paul Trent stood waiting.

Mills thought that he hadn't changed at all since their last meeting, that same stern gaze as though already demanding an apology.

Jane Trent gestured to the detectives to take a seat, and then did so herself, though her husband remained standing.

Mills wondered if either of them knew that Geoff Wormsley had spent time in their home; upstairs with their daughter, some after school psychology but not the kind to be found on any official syllabus.

Tyler was talking, and Mills guessed he wouldn't have to wait long to find out.

He listened as the senior detective explained that their daughter had recently been attending college in Fenton. It seemed to come as a surprise to both of them. They knew the name Wormsley from Stacey's time at college in Shelton, though they had never actually met the man. Mills wondered which way Tyler would go.

"Jon Kelly?" said Tyler. The name again drew a blank from both parents. Mills watched as Tyler wrestled silently with something, and Paul Trent's growing impatience settled like a blanket of radiation over the room. At last Tyler said, "Were you ever approached for money?"

"Are you suggesting ..?" Trent's eyes glowed with latent anger. "Are you saying that our daughter's murder was to do with money?"

Tyler repeated the question. Jane Trent was looking at her husband. "Paul?" she said.

Trent swallowed. And then he sat down. "Stacey rang me."

"When was this?" asked Tyler.

"It was ... a few days before she died."

"Paul, why didn't you say anything -?"

"She asked me for money. I told her, I said she could come back home any time she wanted. I told her she was always welcome."

"Paul, why -"

Trent exploded; back up on his feet, glaring at his wife. "I wasn't going to fund the life she was living. I didn't know what the money was for and to be honest I didn't want to know. If she had enough of that life, she knew she could come back home, the door was always open."

"But you should have told me, Paul. We should have discussed it."

"There was nothing to discuss. She asked for money and I told her to come home."

Silence lingered in the echoes for a few moments, and then Tyler said, "Did she ring again?"

"Yes, she rang again, she rang three times in all, rang my office; and I told her the same thing every time."

"Why - ?" started his wife.

"Didn't she ring *you*? Because she has the sense to know that I'm the one with his hands on the purse strings around here." He made it sound like an accusation.

"She asked for a substantial sum?" asked Tyler.

"She didn't specify. But by the nature of the call, and out of the blue like that, she was hardly asking for money to buy ice cream."

The bitterness came out raw and savage. Trent turned on his wife. "She had everything her little heart desired, she only had to ask and it was there on a plate. Ludicrous expense for little rich girl's toys."

"Paul!"

"It's true. You spoiled her and look at the thanks you got, look what she became? She didn't know the value of anything. Well, most of the money that's been coming in all these years was on my account. And these days that's where it stays!"

A garish smile accompanied his poor joke, and then he sat back down. The tears were bubbling in the corners of his eyes, and then he folded over, his head in his hands, loud sobs emerging, filling the room with their harrowing tones. Once the storm had passed, he looked up. "Are you saying ... you know what the money was for? Was someone using my daughter to get at my money?"

"We're looking into all possibilities," said Tyler.

"Those were the kinds of people she was choosing to consort with. Why, what did we ever do?"

Jane Trent spoke up, her voice quivering. "Someone killed our daughter because you wouldn't ..."

"What – because I wouldn't throw any more money at her, or at whoever was pulling her strings?" He looked back at Tyler. "You mentioned a name earlier."

"Jon Kelly," said Tyler.

"Who is he – some boyfriend she was involved with? Are you saying he was behind my daughter's request for money?"

"Was she in some kind of trouble?" asked Jane Trent. "Was someone threatening Stacey, was this Kelly threatening our daughter?"

Mills drove back towards the city. Tyler sat rigid in the passenger seat, brooding over the case. "*West End Girls*," he said at last.

They pulled up outside and Tyler rang the bell. A woman he hadn't seen before opened the door and greeted him with a smile. She scarcely looked old enough to be there. He flashed his ID and she took a step backward.

"Hayley Greener?" he said.

"She's in the back," said the young woman.

"I know the way."

Mills followed the DCI through the corridor to the office at the rear of the building. Greener was on the phone. Tyler took a seat opposite and gestured to Mills to close the door. The call ended abruptly.

"What can I do for you today?" Greener asked.

"Jon Kelly." Her look betrayed her. "Tell me about your relationship with Kelly," said Tyler.

According to Greener, there wasn't much to tell. He'd introduced a few of the women and they'd been taken on. "I don't like the word 'pimp'," she said, "I think more in terms of 'agent' actually. Some of the workers here have been a bit keen on the substances, if you take my meaning, and that can lead to all kinds of muddled thinking. You need a clear head when it comes to negotiating terms and conditions. There's nothing more to it."

"He introduced Christine Rayworth?"

"Yes, he did."

"And Stacey?"

"That was Christine, like I already told you. They knew each other, I think from working the beat on Waterloo Road and down in Eleanor Street."

"And what about Paul and Jane Trent?" said Tyler.

"Excuse me?" Tyler looked at her, waiting for her to respond. "I take it they are related?" Her tone had an edge of sarcasm, but it was restrained, somewhat tentative.

"Care to guess the relationship?" said Tyler.

"Do you mind telling me what this is all about?"

"I can sum it up in a word, if I need to."

"You're talking in riddles. Am I supposed to have any -"

"*Money.*"

"Could you be more specific?" said Greener.

"It doesn't seem to be any secret that she had wealthy parents."

Greener's laughter rang loud and hollow. "Whoa," she said, "I don't like the way this is going. I wonder if I shouldn't have some legal representation here in this room."

"If you wish," said Tyler, "and we could take it down to the station. Or else we could keep things informal, for the moment at least."

"You're not making accusations?"

"I'm trying to establish facts."

"And you reckon someone was trying to extort money from Stacey's parents?" Greener nodded. "I can see how that might work," she said. "And you're thinking Jon Kelly?"

She sat back in her chair. "Let me tell you something."

"I'm listening," said Tyler.

"This can be a dirty business, it goes without saying, and I've come across a lot of people who belong in the gutter, and some I might even go a lot further and describe as belonging in the ground. But that does not, contrary to some public perceptions, relate to the entire industry. And that's what it is, at the end of the day, it's an industry, it's a business; and like any business you come across all sorts, you work with and meet honest people, some desperate ones, and you meet some bad apples too."

"What are you trying to say?" asked Tyler.

"I'm saying that I have standards. I'm saying that I try to run a fair business, make a living, have a decent working environment for my girls and take some pride in the service we offer. I didn't deserve to have my business burned to the ground because the previous owners happened to run a sweet shop before I arrived there. They're trying to turn that woman into a hero, and it stinks. It's a strange world we're living in when you can torch someone's business and they want to make you a saint."

Greener shook her head. "But that's another story. Doubtless you don't care much about my livelihood being razed to the ground. You'd probably turn a blind eye if she came down here with a can of petrol and shut me down altogether. As for Jon Kelly – you might not want to take him home to meet your mother, but I've always found him a reasonable man to deal with. Christine hates him because the word is he was at least two-timing her. But you go with a man like Kelly, you have to know what you're getting, surely to God."

"What about Christine?" said Tyler.

"What about her? You think she might have been after the Trent money?" Greener shrugged. "Wouldn't surprise me either way. Nothing would surprise me in fact. They might have been queuing down the street to get a piece of the action for all I know."

Greener eased forward again in her chair, her sharp eyes resting full bore on Tyler. "But before you say it, let me tell you this for nothing: I run a legitimate business. I don't diversify; this is a tight ship and whether you can stomach it or not, I provide a valuable service in this city, and if I'm approached to launder or any other dirty work, I'm not interested. My books are transparent, you've seen them, and you're always welcome to see them again, any time, day or night. I don't get involved in the buying and selling of drugs, but neither am I some puritan crusader who insists the workers are clean. They have their lives, and some of them have their problems, most of them, one way or another, like most people, in most businesses.

"If Christine is so messed up she would kill her friend because she was seeing Kelly or because she was trying to work some scheme to fleece Stacey Trent's folks that she couldn't bring off – I can't answer for that."

As the detectives were leaving the premises a familiar figure was coming in the door. He didn't appear to recognise them.

"Hello, Mr Hately," said Mills.

"Is Scarlet in?" said Hately. "She's not been around much and I'm missing her."

The young woman who had answered the door to the detectives earlier, came down the corridor to greet him. "Hi, Roy! You've come to see Scarlet?"

His eyes lit brightly. "Is she back?"

"I'm afraid not, sorry. But I've got some time, if you'd like to come through."

Mills watched the old man follow the young woman hungrily down the corridor, and then he stepped outside to breathe in some much needed fresh air.

"Everything alright?" Tyler asked him.

"Just having a moment," said Mills.

"I know what you mean."

"What now?"

"I'd say enough for today. Let's resume tomorrow, eh?"

Mills didn't need any persuading, and he drove the two of them back to Cedar Lane, before heading home.

But Tyler still had one more visit in mind.

CHAPTER THIRTY SEVEN

Lillistock looked surprised to see the DCI back on her doorstep so soon.

"Coffee?" she asked after showing him inside.

"Why not? Your last shift tomorrow?"

"That's right."

"Do you have anything lined up for the future?"

"As a matter of fact, yes, I have."

She disappeared to make the drinks, and brought them through. "But kind of you though it is to ask, I'm sure you're not here out of concern for my next career move."

"Not entirely, no," he said, before taking a sip of his drink. "The last time we spoke ..."

"You asked a lot of questions about Stacey, and I told you as much as I know."

"And you told me about Kelly and Greener, but you didn't know the name Dean Stewart."

"You said he was another one of Stacey's boyfriends. I tell you, that girl got around, even by the standards of this game, and that's saying something. But I still don't recognise the name."

"You said that Stacey once made a comment about being able to leave this business any time she wanted, because she had, as I think you quoted, 'Mummy and Daddy to go back to.'"

"That's right; she said that, more or less. She said a lot of things, and a lot of the girls didn't like her for it. The last thing you need, when you're in this line of work because you don't have many options, and you're living hand to mouth – the last thing you need is someone rubbing your face in it and telling you it's all a bit of a rich girl's playtime."

"Good motives for murder," said Tyler.

"I'd say that was a bit strong. But you never know."

"Was there anyone who seemed to be particularly wound up by Stacey's attitude?"

"No-one stands out. I know she was close to Christine, but then I also heard they might have been fighting over Kelly. So you can draw your own conclusions."

"You keep your ear to the ground," said Tyler.

"I try to. You hear a lot of things that way, but you don't always have to believe them."

"Like the fact that Stacey may have had plans to extort money?"

"I knew something was in the air. I didn't know the details. Haven't we already covered this?"

"I want to try and narrow it down."

"I imagine that is your job." She took a drink from her cup. "There was talk of her going back to college, I heard that. And when I heard rumours she left college because a teacher had come on strong, I put two and two together. You think her and Kelly maybe?" She took another drink. "Or is this where the other guy comes in, this ..?"

"Dean Stewart," said Tyler. "But I want to get more specific. Stacey's parents."

"I don't know a lot about them, except that they're supposed to be loaded."

"Maybe that's all you need to know."

"Plans to get money from them? Stacey, you mean?" Her eyes glowed. "What a bitch."

"You heard nothing about that?"

198

"Not until now." Her eyes narrowed onto the detective. "Wait a minute, why are you sharing this?"

Tyler finished his drink. "Some detectives, with more suspicious minds than mine, might question why you are choosing now to leave the profession. They might begin to wonder if you have suddenly come into some money, and can afford to take a career break, and do something else."

He watched her carefully as she placed her empty cup down on the table.

"How else can I put this," she said. She held up a finger. "Firstly, someone sets fire to my place of work." She held up a second finger. "Someone murders one of my colleagues. Are you getting the picture?"

"You've painted it for me already."

"Maybe that's because it's an honest depiction of how it is. The writing's on the wall, and I want out. A wake up call or however else you want to phrase it."

He looked at her as long moments ticked in the silence of the flat. A corner appeared to have been turned, and at last Tyler eased back. "Okay," he said. "Then I want to ask a favour."

"What kind of favour?"

"They're short staffed at the moment, on account of some of the reasons you've already suggested."

"You're not recruiting?"

"Along those lines."

"Now I've heard it all!"

"A few extra shifts ..."

"I thought you used your own undercover officers."

"You just can't get the staff these days."

Lillistock was shaking her head. "I don't believe we're even having this conversation."

"I'm not sure I believe it myself."

"What – you think I can ask a few questions and someone will confess to me that they killed Stacey?"

"If only life and this job were so easy," said Tyler.

"Then ... I don't understand."

"All I'm asking is that you keep your ear to the ground for a few days."

"You've got some nerve, I'll give you that."

"I've found," said Tyler, "that if you don't ask you don't get."

He went outside and stood by his car, looking back towards the flat. It was getting on into the evening. Stewart had about half an hour left on his shift.

CHAPTER THIRTY EIGHT

Tyler found Mr Tideswell in his office, the manager practically swooning when he saw the detective arrive.

"What – back again? I wonder if you haven't got a thing going with one of our checkout girls."

"Not this week," said Tyler.

"I take it you've come to see our Mr Stewart."

"You have psychic skills. How's he been getting on?"

"He's a decent lad. If he wanted a reference it would be glowing - and this despite your best efforts, DCI Tyler. Is this still about the murder?"

"I'm afraid so."

"I thought you got someone for that?" Then he smacked the side of his head. "No, that's right: she only burned the brothel down! And I hear they want to make her mayor." He issued a burst of dry laughter and snorted. "Mind you, at least she takes action, which is more than can be said of the incumbent. All he ever does is get fat on free lunches and dance around in a chain and fancy dress."

"Stewart's about to finish his shift," said Tyler.

Tideswell checked the clock above his desk. "Is that the time already? No wonder I'm feeling old. He'll be done in ten minutes. Feel free to take a seat."

Tyler took up the offer, and waited for the obligatory question.

"So," said Tideswell, "any closer to finding the culprit?"

"We're working on it. Out of interest, have you seen Mr Stewart with anyone in particular lately?"

"What, like a woman, you mean?"

"Yes. *Like a woman.*"

"I can't say that I have."

"I see. Word tends to get around in a place like this," said Tyler.

Tideswell smiled. "You're after an update? I know just the person," he said. "Give me two minutes, and while I'm gone I'll make sure Stewart hangs back after his shift ends."

The manager was as good as his word. He returned to his office and sat back down in his chair. "She's a good one is Tara. Nothing she can't tell you about the staff here. And, as luck would have it, she specialises in affairs of the heart. We have a few on our payroll who have skills in that department, so we are truly blessed. Anyway, as far as she knows, our friend is currently unattached, and in celebration of this fact a couple of the girls have their eye on him. A popular lad – isn't it great to be young and popular? Of course, I wouldn't know about the last bit, and I only have a dim memory of the first bit, now I come to think about it."

There was a knock at the door. "Come in," Tideswell shouted, his voice full of good cheer. Stewart walked in and stopped dead when he saw Tyler. "Take a seat," said Tideswell. "No need to be shy." Stewart sat down. "DCI Tyler would like to -"

"Yes, thank you," said Tyler. "I believe we can take it from here."

"Ah, yes, of course," said Tideswell, getting up. "You'll be wanting some privacy now, I expect. Use my office anytime; you don't even need to ask."

After the door had closed behind the manager, Tyler said, "I'm sorry to trouble you again."

"I'm getting used to it. What can I tell you now?"

"Jon Kelly. What was his relationship with Stacey Trent?"

Stewart rolled his eyes. "I told you, I stopped seeing her ..."

"That's not what I asked. Kelly was her pimp?"

"Was he? I didn't know that. But so what if he was?"

"Her parents were wealthy, did you know *that*?"

Stewart recoiled at the vehemence in the detective's voice. "I knew they had money. Stacey told me. She also told me she didn't want anything to do with them."

"Did she tell you why she didn't want anything to do with them?"

"She said they were control freaks, and that she wanted to live her own life."

Tyler looked at Stewart, and kept looking. "If someone, perhaps someone close to Stacey, put pressure on her, pressure to ask her wealthy parents for money ..."

"Are you accusing me of something?"

"Suppose someone did that, though. Who do you reckon would be most likely? Who would be the likely candidate to exert that kind of pressure? And who do you reckon might take things further if the parents refused to give her money?"

"I've no idea," said Stewart.

"You look afraid of something," said Tyler. "Who are you afraid of – me?"

"I've done nothing wrong."

"But you have your suspicions, don't you? So, let's make a few suggestions, and try to work this little puzzle out, shall we?"

"I don't know anything, I told you."

"Jon Kelly?" said Tyler. "Christine Rayworth? How about one of the other workers at *The Sweet Box*, or *West End Girls*? Who would you put your money on?"

Stewart was starting to sweat. If he was going to crack, thought Tyler, this was it, this was the moment.

"I didn't like any of them. I didn't know them, but sometimes we'd be out having a drink and these characters would come over. I wish I never met Stacey, it was a mistake. I fancied her, she was great fun, and I'd never met anyone like her before. But then I realised what she was, how she was, and I didn't want any part of it."

"But you knew about the plan to use Stacey to get at her parents' money."

"This is the first I've heard about it."

"Did you know any of the other women?"

"I met one or two – like I said, these characters would be knocking about when I was out with Stacey. I work in Stoke and I went for drinks with her around the town."

"May Lillistock?"

"I don't know - I didn't know the names."

"You met Hayley Greener?"

"Stacey mentioned her. I didn't meet her."

Tyler kept on looking at Stewart. Then he said, "I'm sorry I've wasted your time this evening."

He followed Stewart out of the office and Tideswell was waiting around the corner.

"All done?" the manager asked, cheerfully, nodding at Stewart and then at Tyler. "Same time tomorrow, is it?"

Tyler got into his car and waited for Stewart to drive away. He followed him back to Hanley, to the flats where he lived. It didn't seem likely that Stewart had clocked him. Tyler drove around the corner and waited, willing something to happen.

An hour later, he gave it up and went home.

CHAPTER THIRTY NINE

Mills couldn't settle. His children had gone up to bed and his wife was taking a bath. He put on a CD, the one his kids had bought for him last Christmas. A band from his youth, his days of longer hair and a flatter stomach, and he had worn the grooves down on the vinyl version long before he had met his future wife. But listening now to music that had once made him feel glad to be alive, all it was doing was to make him feel older and more restless than ever.

He switched the music off and flicked on the TV. He couldn't think to music anymore; the background hum of news somehow provoked his imagination better than the inevitable drifting back into the past that accompanied the tunes he had grown up with.

The carousel of faces and names from the last few days whirred in and out of consciousness, but there was no focus to be found anywhere. On a whim, without thinking it through, he rang Tyler. There was no answer. He gave it five minutes and tried again, but still there was no response.

He plonked himself back in front of the TV, his feet tapping the floor to some inaudible beat. How was Tyler spending the evening, he wondered. What strange concoctions were floating through that peculiar mind? Was he out there stamping the pavements, putting in the miles until it killed him? The DCI's mood had been hard to gauge lately, and some of his thinking hard to fathom. The warning signs were there, bright as day and at the same time as obscure as midnight fog. But the darker the DCI's moods, generally the less he was likely to discuss them. That was the pattern, and it was hardly unique; the man was a loner, an enigma, damaged and at the same time priceless. *"What are you up to right now?"* whispered Mills. *"What suicide mission ... what career wrecking ..."*

He went through to the hallway again and picked up the handset. This time Tyler answered.

"I've been back to see Stewart. I had the notion that ... I don't know."

"Are you alright, Jim?"

"Never better, since you ask: sound of body and mind, against all odds, and yet still I can't seem to get any purchase on this one. My instincts have all but deserted me and I feel too damned tired to sleep."

"Why did you go back to see Stewart?"

"Desperation, Danny. He's the odd one in the pack; he's the one I can least fathom. Stacey Trent's boyfriend - and he seemed too good to be true; and at the same time mixed up with all the wrong people and denying knowing any of them. Am I making any sense?"

"Not much," admitted Mills.

"That's what I thought. But I had this conviction that if I kept scraping away at it, something would peel off and be revealed. Just an inch below the surface, less than that, but I could practically feel it waiting down there for me to find it."

"What are you talking about, Jim?"

"This is all about Trent's family – or should I say their money. Stewart – what, coercing her, threatening her, forcing her in some way to go after the golden pot; nothing doing chasing Wormsley and his string of debts, so move on to the star prize?"

"Isn't that more Jon Kelly's game?"

"It might be at that. But that seems too obvious. I can never settle for the obvious, Danny, you know me better than that. I even wondered if her old flame, Kev, was still around or back from his Spanish travels. But whatever, whoever, I can't make it fit. She rings her father ... she asks for money ... he says no ... and so someone angry and frustrated at the lack of a result carves her up in a park. Who would choose to do that? Tell me I'm barking up the wrong tree."

But Mills had no answers. He felt the weight of his own impotence as he struggled to find something to say.

"What this person did to her, Danny, it suggests rage. Yet what would provoke that degree of rage?"

Mills listened.

"... Val Hackett acted out of rage, rage born out of grief ... perhaps after all she was so far out of her mind that she could cut someone's face to ribbons. Or Wormsley, out of his mind with fear, flips and decides it's time to end all possibility that she might come back should he ever find himself back on his feet. But I don't believe any of these scenarios, not really, and so I pluck out the name Dean Stewart and I go after him, trusting to luck that the slightest of hunches might turn something up."

Mills could hear the desperation in Tyler's voice, but he knew there was still more to come.

"I went to see May Lillistock. I had a feeling that she and Stewart might have concocted the plot to go after the Trents' money. I based that on sheer gut feeling. I've been out pushing buttons blindly, Danny, hoping that bells might yet start to ring."

"What do you mean, Jim?"

"Lillistock is quitting the job. She's bright, knows how the world works, or a part of it. I could see her and Stewart, two of a kind. I let my imagination get the better of me."

"*Jim?*"

"Tomorrow night is her final scheduled shift at *West End Girls*. I asked her to stay on a little longer."

"You did what?"

"I know."

"Jim, for God's sake! Listen to me: I'm coming over."

"No point. I'm going out."

"Where now – who?"

"Don't panic, the damage is done. I'm going out to try and run some of this off, and regain some sanity. I've no further visits planned."

"What did Lillistock say?"

"She didn't, not really. I thought I might follow Stewart to her flat and wrap everything up in one evening's work, presentable to a chief superintendant. I was away with the fairies, Danny. I have little doubt that Carstairs will hear about my dabblings, and so hear me when I tell you that you don't know about any of this."

Mills started to speak, but Tyler cut in. "I've said more than enough and I need to get some miles in, and then we'll see what the morning brings."

He ended the call. Mills could hear his wife coming down the stairs. He placed the receiver back on its cradle and looked up. "Nice bath?" he said.

"Is everything alright?" she asked him.

"It will be."

"Want to talk about it?"

Mills followed her into the lounge. He told her what he hadn't already, and she listened intently. "You're both doing your best," she said once he'd finished talking. "You can't do more than that."

"That's what we tell the kids," said Mills.

"And that's because it's true."

"Jim always takes it personally. He doesn't get a result, and he gets it into his head it's because he isn't trying hard enough, or that he isn't good enough. He can't seem to shake that. It goes back to his childhood, but knowing it doesn't seem to help him deal with it."

"Danny, if you've no evidence to work with ... maybe he's trying too hard."

"That's Jim for you. But try telling him. He's trying to put the puzzle together with half the pieces missing, and still blaming himself when nothing fits."

"I'm no detective, but what if it was a random attack, someone unknown to the victim? A predator who just happened to be there that night and saw a potential victim."

"But why would a predator carve her up like that?"

"I don't know, Danny. But it happens; there are some very sick people out there."

"Tell me about it."

"You can't always find an explanation for the things people do, you know that." She placed a hand on his arm and then she kissed him. "What are you going to do?"

"What can I do? Jim's the senior officer; he doesn't listen to me when he's in one of these moods. He goes his own way and God alone knows what he's going to do. There's a self destruct button wired into him, and he keeps pressing at the bloody thing."

*

Tyler ran through the quiet streets of Penkhull village, breathing hard against the night, his pace relentless. His head was splitting, images of the dead girl, faces and names spinning behind his eyes, blurring into a landscape of confusion. Without choosing a direction, he found himself heading into Stoke, cutting through into Shelton and then out on the long drag to Hanley, passing Cedar Lane, and down into Northwood. A part of him knew where he was going; pulled him through the streets with a force of gravity, back towards the flat near to the stadium where May Lillistock lived alone.

He hit Meerside Walk before his location had fully registered in the conscious part of his brain; and there it was, parked on the far side of the street, just beyond the entrance to the flats.

Dean Stewart's old Fiesta.

*

Mills lay in bed staring at the ceiling, staring through the darkness. He pictured Tyler tearing through the city, stopping to hammer on doors, and winding up everyone he could find until the entire city was sitting up in anger. And then he saw Carstairs chewing him out, answering complaints by the dozen: suspension, disgrace, kicked off the force and disappearing back into a bottle to live out the remainder of his days in the gutter.

"Get a grip," he murmured, and felt his wife stir beside him and then fall back into soft snores. "Get a bloody grip," he muttered again. But he couldn't be sure if he was addressing himself or Tyler or both.

*

Tyler stood beneath a mercilessly hot shower. His body ached from the exertion of the run, but he still felt he could crawl up the walls.

211

At last he lay on the bed and closed his eyes. He sensed that all his wires were crossed. Were Stewart and Lillistock conspiring to work Trent to get at her parents' fortune? Was Kelly involved at all, or had he merely aspired to be?

The internal jury that operated behind Tyler's eyes was still out regarding Rayworth, who, he admitted to himself, was another one that he just couldn't fathom.

He eased without knowing it into an edgy sleep, mistaking dream for the waking world, and seeing the figures dressed in black, the villains society had long endorsed haunting his schooldays, the orphan navigating the monsters of childhood, summoned to the midnight study to receive his medicine.

He woke with a start, wanting a drink, something hard and bitter, wanting to fight, for Carstairs to come at him all guns blazing, and then unload, the death of nightmare focused into a single punch to the brain.

CHAPTER FORTY

Mills was at his desk early, feeling like he hadn't been to bed. Carstairs sprang across the floor of the CID office.

"Do you know anything about this?" he said.

"About what, sir?" asked Mills.

"I've got complaints coming out of the walls."

Mills raised his eyebrows. "Sir?"

"Were you doing the rounds with DCI Tyler last evening?"

"I wasn't, sir."

"Not visiting Lillistock or Stewart, by any chance?"

"No, sir."

Carstairs appeared to steady himself. "Please inform DCI Tyler that I wish to speak to him urgently." He left the office as decisively as he had entered it.

"*What have you done, Jim*?" said Mills. On cue Tyler strode into the office, appearing perky and untroubled. "Carstairs was looking for you. He's on the war path, so be warned. He wants a word."

"I don't doubt it for a second. Does he not think I have work to be getting on with?"

"How did your run go?"

Tyler eyed the DS. "Is that really an enquiry into how I spent my evening, or are you wondering if I was out digging a grave for myself to fall into?" While Mills was working out his response, Tyler said, "Stewart was out visiting Lillistock late last night."

"I see," said Mills.

"Meaning?"

"You went back."

"Your disapproval is clear to see."

"There have been complaints," said Mills.

"I bet there have," said Tyler, smiling. "I would have been disappointed if there hadn't been."

"What are you playing at?"

"I want to see how far I can push those two before they finally crack."

But before Mills could say anything more Tyler was already heading down the corridor towards the chief inspector's office.

"Been nice working with you, Jim ..."

*

Carstairs looked solemn indeed. "I won't beat about the bush. I've received two more complaints about you."

"Anyone we know?"

"Lillistock – does the name mean anything?"

"It most certainly does."

"Then perhaps you can explain why you visited her, repeatedly, and requested that she continue working at *West End Girls.*" Tyler hesitated. "Well, DCI Tyler?"

"It's ... hard to explain."

"I'm sure it is. But I strongly suggest that you have a stab at it!"

"I'm hedging my bets," said Tyler at last. "I can't make my mind up about Lillistock. But I'm convinced that the solution to this case lies at *West End Girls.* I also happen to believe she is in cahoots with Stewart. I wanted to test the waters."

"Did you? You're not making much sense. Cahoots over what, exactly?"

"Attempts to coerce Stacey Trent to extract money?"

"From ..?"

"Her parents, and possibly from Wormsley."

"I thought that was Jon Kelly territory."

"That's a common perception. It still might be the case."

"So why – and this brings me to the second complaint of the day so far – are you hounding Stewart, when you have, as far as I understand it, absolutely no evidence against him whatsoever." But before Tyler could answer, Carstairs issued a warning. "And don't you dare to tell me that it's all down to the detective's hunch."

"Alright."

"Alright what?"

"I won't put it in those terms. But Stewart and Lillistock have complained because I'm getting too close for comfort. It's what I expected them to do."

"It confirms nothing! It confirms that you were out of order, and scratching around on misguided notions about gut feelings. We can't afford loose cannons rolling around in this department. I want your final report and then you're off the case, and I don't mind informing you that I'm looking at suspension of duties."

The moment hung on a thread. And then something changed. Tyler, looking deep into the eyes of Chief Superintendent Carstairs, failed to recognise the monsters that had plagued his past, the authoritarian bullies who had first placed him onto the path of self destruction. Instead he saw a variation of Graham Berkins, and felt the clenched fists at his sides unfurl.

"Is there something else you wish to say?" asked Carstairs.

Tyler shook his head, still processing this latest revelation. He walked back to the CID office and sat down at his desk. Mills had gone out. He started on his report.

Mills parked outside *West End Girls* and rang the bell. Greener answered the door.

"Comes to something," she said. "You buy a pack of dogs and end up doing the barking yourself. Come through."

Mills followed her to the office at the back of the building. She pointed to the seat by her desk and he took it.

"Bit short staffed?"

"A *bit*? Word gets around that they're closing us down, and they're all back working the streets even before the axe has fallen. Comradeship, loyalty – I expect too much, I know. We were doing alright until that mad piece of work decided to torch *The Sweet Box*. Now everyone has a new cause: close down the brothels, make her mayor, and the council – still undecided which way the cookie's going to crumble, and playing it safe as usual - are running scared and making life difficult. We're on borrowed time and all the girls know it."

She offered the DS a weary smile. "Anyway, you wanted to speak to me."

"Geoff Wormsley," he said.

"I don't know that name."

"Jon Kelly, Christine Rayworth, Dean Stewart, May Lillistock ..."

"What is this?" asked Greener. "Some new quiz you're trying out? I don't think it's going to catch on, but then I'm an old fashioned kind of girl with old fashioned tastes. What's going on?"

"You tell me."

"If you're looking for character references, okay, and maybe if I scratch your back, you'll put in a word

216

for me and help bail out some of the water around here, because I'm sinking, and fast. I'm doing my best with what I've got, but I can't service the entire needs of a city single handed."

"Let's see."

"In any particular order?"

"That's entirely your call."

"I'll go with the order you gave me, then. Isn't this fun! So, Jon Kelly: It's no secret, he puts work my way; he gets around, fingers in pies and other things besides. He used to tell me that he road tests every girl he introduces to me, his guarantee of satisfaction. If there's money to be made, and a place to put his dick, Jon Kelly doesn't need any second invitation. He was going with Christine and I'd say with Stacey too. And that was always bound to cause trouble.

"As for Christine, what more can I say? She seemed close to Stacey, and if that was because she had designs on her folks' money, I wouldn't claim to be surprised. She had a rough upbringing, and she seemed the type to carry a grudge. If Kelly was two-timing her for the little rich girl, I could see things turning nasty."

"And what about the others?" asked Mills.

"I didn't know Stewart, but I heard Stacey was keen on him. But Stacey was keen on a lot of men. She could never get enough, and it makes sense to me that most boyfriends might quickly get tired of that. Kelly was always out for what he could get, and he knew the deal. If he was messing with the likes of Stacey and even Christine, but especially Stacey, he was too worldly–wise to expect commitment. But what I hear of Stewart, he was outside this game; he might have thought he was buying into glamour when he met Stacey, but once he knew what she was like ..."

"What was she like?"

Greener switched on the kettle.

"She wasn't like any of the others. I'll be honest – and I don't say this often, but I couldn't fathom her. She came from a different place, and she fascinated me. I don't even mean because she had wealthy parents, I mean her mind set, the way she was."

"Can you explain what you mean?" asked Mills.

"I can try to. It's like when she was Scarlet, this alter ego, it would kind of take over, like she was playing a part, but at the same time you couldn't see the other part of her. She inhabited the role, or else it inhabited her. Some of the clients loved it, and they would ask for her and some wouldn't see any of the other girls, it had to be her. Maybe she missed her vocation; perhaps she should have been on the stage. Or maybe she was just messed up beyond hope. It was hard to get the measure. I never got near."

Greener made two mugs of tea and handed one to Mills.

"You know that song, *Common People*. I always thought of that: like she was playing at this life, playing a game."

"You're not the first person I've heard make that observation."

Greener looked at Mills and then laughed. "It's fucking hilarious really, when you stop to think about it."

"How do you mean?"

"Oh, come on. If all of this is down to someone having designs on her folks' money – you couldn't make it up! You'll have all the professors having to come up with new theories on the workings of irony."

"May Lillistock?"

218

"She's another one jumping ship. Her last shift today. She's okay is May, though we've had our differences. I'll be sorry to lose her; very popular with the punters. Mind you, if you're in the habit of keeping secrets, she's the last person you want around. But that's a two way street, I suppose. She's kept me in the loop often enough, and so I shouldn't complain."

"Did she have much to do with the others?"

"May? How do you mean – with the other girls?" Greener's concentrated look at the DS caused him to blanch. "Now I'm curious," she said. "I can understand you asking me about Christine and Kelly, even Stewart, seeing as he was knocking about with Stacey. But what's the angle on May?"

"I'm not sure there is one," said Mills. "We're still making enquiries ..."

But Greener wasn't looking in the least convinced. "No, I don't think so. Is she a person of interest?"

"Like I said, we're -"

"Look, we won't get far if you're not going to level with me." Mills felt himself wilting under the scrutiny of her stare. "Come on, cough it up, whatever it is."

But the truth of the matter was that he was doing nothing more than sounding out a hunch that belonged entirely in the realm of DCI Tyler. So he had found out that Stewart and Lillistock might be an item, so what? It didn't mean anything, necessarily, even if they were being secretive about it.

Greener was grinning. "I can practically see the thoughts running through your head. Care to share them with little old Hayley?"

What the hell, thought Mills. "She might be in a relationship with Stewart," he said.

219

"And you believe that may be significant?" Greener seemed to be trying to fathom something. "Wait a minute, so let me get this straight in my head. Stewart was seeing Stacey, there's some suggestion doing the rounds that either Stacey or someone else was after her parents' money ... am I getting warm? Are you saying May is moving on because she's got bigger fish to fry? That she's hit the jackpot?"

"No, I'm not saying -"

"That Stacey was killed because the plan to get at her folks' money went south, and the killer might have been Stewart or May or both of them?" She laughed. "For what it's worth, my money's still on that psychopath who burned my business down. But there's an agenda in this city to close down businesses like mine, and so while she ought to be doing a good long stretch for what she's done, she's going to end up mayor and no doubt knighted in the New Year's ..."

Mills couldn't face another speech and gave it up. Tyler's hunches just didn't stack. He had to concede that it was official: the DCI was losing the plot.

He stood up to leave.

"Anyway, where's your friend today?" Greener said. "A few of the girls have been asking about him. If he's unattached, I think he could be popular around here."

"I'll let him know that," said Mills.

"You do that. And you put that mad bitch behind bars where she belongs, and let decent people get on and run their business."

She walked him to the door.

"Thanks for your time," he said, stepping out onto the pavement.

Greener looked up the street. "God, that's all we need."

Mills recognised the figure of Ron Hately coming down towards them. "Still asking to see Scarlet?"

"Isn't he ever? He's up to four times a day now, asking if she's in. Sad, really, I suppose. Is that what my life has come down to, servicing the likes of him?"

"Does he stay?"

"He might come in and chat with one of the girls, depending who's on. He's obviously lonely. Some days he turns around and goes home, and maybe turns up again later. Four times a day, though - it's no joke."

"Hi, Mr Hately," said Greener.

"I've come to see Scarlet. Is she back yet?"

"Sorry, she's not."

He offered a mournful attempt at a smile. "Oh, well, tell her I'll call back later, then." And with that he turned around and headed back up the street towards his house.

"Poor bastard," said Greener.

"He never causes any bother?"

"None at all, bless. They've started sending a social worker or health visitor or someone round. I've got a friend in that line of work, and you can't figure them out."

"Can't figure who out?" asked Mills.

"The social I mean. On the one hand you've got the council talking about closing places like mine down, and on the other I've heard of them giving out direct payments to men like him. 'Go and have a good shag on the NHS, Roy!' Not very joined up thinking, is it?"

Mills took the opportunity to say his goodbyes and climbed back into his car. He watched Hately disappear into the house and then he glanced back as Greener closed the door of *West End Girls*. He didn't know if she was talking rubbish about funding lonely old men

221

to use the local brothels, but he'd been around long enough to know that only a fool would put anything past the local authority.

A sense of foreboding overtook him as he drove back to Cedar Lane, his thoughts turning to how Tyler had gone on with Carstairs.

CHAPTER FORTY ONE

Tyler was seated at his desk, writing up his final report on the case. He looked up when he saw Mills come in, and offered him a thin smile. Mills knew the DCI well enough to recognise that look. "As bad as that?"

"Oh, I don't know. I have my health and strength, and as far as I know, from the last time I looked, the world is still turning. How bad can it be?" Mills waited to find out. "Carstairs wants to take me off the case. I can't say I blame him. I've been chasing shadows and it's time for fresh eyes and clearer instincts. For once, Danny, I'm not complaining. I feel like a load has been taken off me."

Mills offered a look and it was one tinged with scepticism.

"Look at me how you like and for as long as you like, but I'm telling you how it is, and it's the truth."

"He's reassigning you to other duties?"

"That's still to be decided. I've attracted a lot of complaints lately, and I'm seen as a liability. If Carstairs is made permanent he will want me out, that's pretty much a given. But the news is that Berkins is itching to come back. It's a throw of the dice."

"I've never been a gambling man, sir."

"Unlike Geoff Wormsley. I've checked him out and that's where a lot of his money really did go. He has casino accounts that wouldn't be out of place in Las Vegas. I don't know what he's like as a lecturer, but he was brilliant when it came to losing money."

"So Trent really didn't skin him, then?"

"It seems not. Nor anyone else she may or may not have been in partnership with at the time. And apparently she didn't get anything out of her parents either. All of which leads me back to the conclusion that if there was another party involved - and at this point, feel free to fill in the missing name ..."

"You still think that's why she was killed? Somebody using her to get money from Wormsley and the Trent family, and when she failed -"

"I'd put my pension on someone being involved. I may already have done so. As to whether that person actually killed her ..."

"You don't think it was the sweet shop owner, then?"

"Do you?"

"Not for a minute. And Carstairs doesn't really believe that, does he?"

"He wants a result. He doesn't like complaints. Results on his watch look good; complaints don't. The possibility of using complaints to remove a thorn from the side of this department, well, that has to be another positive result for the likes of Carstairs. On the other hand, I think even he can see that unless Val Hackett can be proved to be completely off her head, which seems, contrary to opinions coming from some quarters, highly unlikely, in my opinion, then it just doesn't make sense for her to target one of the workers. If she wanted to target someone, it would surely have been Greener. The arson attack makes perfect sense, whilst the murder of Stacey Trent in that context makes absolutely none at all. All of which is to say, my fate lies in the hands of Graham Berkins, and it has done ever since I punched the lights out of a senior bully in London and arrived here in this land of blessing and exile. Nothing's really changed, Danny. I will walk the line regardless of results, and we both know that's true."

Tyler's office phone was ringing. It was an internal call. Mills watched the look of surprise on the face of the DCI unfolding as he took it.

"A turn up for the books," said Tyler once the call had ended. "It seems we have a late visitor. Wormsley's come in, and he wants to talk."

CHAPTER FORTY TWO

Geoff Wormsley looked rough. Mills could see the dark shadows beneath the man's eyes, and at least a couple of days' worth of untrimmed stubble covering the usually closely shaven face. He looked crumpled, internally as well as outwardly, and clearly the bearer of a heavy load.

"I understand that you want to talk," said Tyler.

Wormsley nodded, and then followed the detective in the direction of the interview rooms, Mills bringing up the rear.

They sat in the room and the detectives waited for Wormsley to begin. Whatever the burden was, it was weighing the bearer down, and yet the unloading of it looked to Mills like it was coming at a price and was going to take some time. Wormsley was rubbing at his face, more agitated than the DS had seen him. He wondered if a confession was on the cards; if the mystery of Trent's death was going to be solved in this single sitting.

"Would a drink help?" asked Tyler, and Wormsley nodded. Nodding seemed to be his sole form of communication these days, the use of spoken language temporarily beyond his command.

Mills organised a strong coffee, and waited for it to take effect.

"I don't know where to start," said Wormsley at last.

"Take your time," said Tyler. "Start wherever feels right for you."

He nodded again and took another long drink, finishing it off. "Thank you," he said, wiping at his mouth with the back of his hand. "I should have said something before now. I should have said something a long time ago."

His hands were over his face, tears spluttering out between his fingers, his chest convulsing in long, heavy sobs that filled the room.

Tyler and Mills sat and waited, riding out the storm, until finally Wormsley lowered his hands, looked at the detectives, and started to talk.

He took them back two years, when Trent was a student at Shelton college and the affair had started, and once it had started it moved quickly, and before he knew it he was in love, that's how he put it: forbidden love, quite possibly, but still it felt like the real thing. And then her parents were going away, a long anniversary trip they'd planned all year, just the two of them; Florida, the Everglades, the Keys, the trip of a lifetime, or one of them. They didn't do badly when it came to holidays, but Paul Trent had been working flat out, putting in the hours, saving up the time for the trip.

That large house, and just Wormsley and Trent, the time of his life, or that's how it had seemed to him; for a short time, for a few days at least, until the honeymoon ended, and the dynamics and the atmosphere suddenly began to change.

"She used to wake up in the night crying," said Wormsley. "She passed it off at first, wouldn't tell me what was on her mind. I asked if she thought it was wrong, us doing what we were doing under her parents' roof. And that's when it started to come out."

He took some deep breaths, digging all the way down to get at the air, and then shook his head. "I can't believe I sat on all this."

227

"It's alright," said Tyler, "you're talking about it now."

After a few minutes Wormsley continued. "Like I said, I asked if she thought it was wrong, what we were doing, where we were doing it, and then she said that a lot worse had taken place there. *In that house.*"

His hands were over his mouth, pressing hard against his lips. As though he was trying to hold it all back in at the same time that he was desperate to let it all out.

"Did she tell you what had happened there?" prompted Tyler.

Wormsley was back to nodding, his hands still tightly pressed against his mouth.

Tyler waited.

"I don't want to go into the details," said Wormsley, "but ... it concerned her father. The things he had done, disgusting things ... when she was still a child, things she had grown up with, things her mother never knew anything about and probably still doesn't as far as I know."

He took another minute. "I asked her if she planned to do anything about it, get help, go to the police maybe. But she said she just needed to tell somebody. I wondered then if she had seen me as a kind of father figure, choosing me as someone to confide in. I'm ashamed to say this ..."

The tears were brimming again, and a look of contempt and disgust overtook him.

"I felt used – can you believe that? I, me, the great Geoff Wormsley, psychologist by trade ... I felt like this young woman, still not much more than a child, was using *me*. That she had contrived to lure me into an affair with her so that she could take me back to the – to the scene of the crime, and be her confidant, or whatever you want to call it.

"The state of my ego – it defies belief! And you know how I responded? I listened, yes, I listened, I did that. I let her talk. I let her pour it all out, hour after hour. I did that much for her; and then the cold feet ... all I wanted to do was be on my way, out of that place, and to never set foot near it again, or to go near Stacey again."

He was breathing heavily, almost convulsing.

"Are you okay?" asked Mills.

"Am I? I'll tell you what I am – I'm a fucking disgrace, that's what I am. When she'd told me the horror of her childhood, with that monster she had for a father ... all she was to me, if I'm honest ... she was nothing but damaged goods. She was ... *contaminated.* The danger light was flashing and I wanted to be out of there. And that's how it ended, and that's why it ended. I made my excuses, I withdrew and I dumped her, left her alone with her misery. I wanted no further part in it. I wanted nothing else to do with Stacey Trent. I left that night and I never went back."

Wormsley's breathing was beginning to ease, and Mills sat back again.

"All my training, all the years I spent studying psychology, and when I got the chance, the one opportunity – but all I could think of was myself and my reputation and my career. I could see it all in tatters, unravelling, and that was all I cared about.

"She wasn't stupid, far from it. She knew the score. I awaited accusations, had my version of the story ready, but nothing ever transpired; and then she left the college, and still nothing, and after a while I started to believe that I'd got away with it.

229

"And then the guilt finally started to settle in. It seemed I was home free, nothing to fear from my transgressions, and at first I didn't know what I was feeling, what was going on. All those theories, all of those books I'd studied, and they didn't count for a thing when it all concerned me and what was going on inside my own head. I couldn't relate to any of it. Sex was my release, and gambling, and then the gambling took over and I thought about it even more than I thought about the sex, and I knew I was in a hole but I couldn't seem to climb out of it ..."

Tyler spoke: "And then, one evening, Mr Wormsley, one Monday evening Stacey walked back into the classroom."

"That's right. I couldn't believe it. I thought I was seeing things. And everything else I've told you is true: I'd wiped myself out before she had chance to get to me, and there was nothing left. I'm finished, I know that. I've had enough of carrying this around and I don't care what happens next. I've gone off sick and I have no plans to go back, and I'll stand up in court and swear under oath the things Stacey told me about, the things that happened to her, that were done to her, in that family home."

Tyler waited until he was certain that Wormsley had finished.

"And you believe that what she told you – about her father – was true?"

"Why would she lie about it? And anyway, the way it came out, the way she told it, I had no reason not to believe her. I still believe her. I could let myself off the hook and try to convince myself that she was making it all up, soften the blow that way, but I don't believe that, not for a second. She was telling me the truth, and I'd put my life on it."

"And you didn't kill her?" said Tyler.

"No, I didn't kill her. I did nothing to help her, but I didn't kill her."

CHAPTER FORTY THREE

Paul Trent answered the door.

"What now?" he said looking out at the detectives.

"We have some more questions for you," said Tyler.

Making no attempt to show them through into the house, Trent said, "What questions?" Before Tyler could respond, Trent added, "I've a question for you: have you found out yet who killed my daughter?"

For a few moments a standoff took place out on the doorstep, and then Tyler said, "Where were you on the night that your daughter was killed, Mr Trent?"

The effect of the question, thought Mills, was something akin to watching footage of a bomb exploding. In the immediate aftermath of the flash, there was a split second of frozen silence, before the ensuing sound rushed back in.

"What are you talking about – what is this?" The voice thundered, an angry, roaring noise focused on the detective. Tyler calmly repeated the question, and then asked if they might enter the house.

Trent walked them through into the lounge, but no-one took a seat. For the third time Tyler asked the question, and this time Trent answered.

"I have no idea what the hell this is about, but believe me, I will be making a complaint, *DCI Tyler*, because I consider it a bloody outrage that you turn up on my doorstep like this, on the doorstep of a man grieving after his daughter has been ...

"But for your information, on the night of Stacey's murder, I was at home with my wife. Now, does that answer your question?"

"I would like to speak to your wife, Mr Trent," said Tyler. "Is she home?"

"As a matter of fact, no, she isn't."

"Do you know when she will be returning?"

Trent's face was twisted in an attitude of rage. "If you must know, she won't be returning."

He turned his back on the detectives, and Tyler looked at Mills.

"Mr Trent?" said Tyler.

"She's left me," said Trent, his back still turned. "The strain of this ... she's gone, walked out." He was shaking, his voice quivering; he was fighting to stay in control.

"Any idea where we might find her?"

"You can try her mother's. That's the usual retreat." He gave the detectives the address.

"Mr Trent," said Tyler, "you told us that Stacey approached you for money. Did anyone else approach you?"

He turned back around to face them. "Like who?"

"Was someone attempting to blackmail you?"

Trent opened his mouth, and then hesitated. "No," he said.

"The obvious question, I would have thought, Mr Trent, is *blackmailing over what*?"

He looked rattled, but he was keeping it out of his voice, back in control, speaking with calm authority. "I've no idea what you're talking about. But if you need to talk to my wife, to 'establish my alibi', then I've told you where you can find her."

He showed the detectives to the door, offering his parting shot as they left: "And you can expect to be hearing from my solicitors."

Tyler got in the car next to Mills. "Quite a collection of complaints I'm building up. I wonder if there's a record for that kind of thing, and perhaps a certificate to go out to the winner. I'll keep a space just above my bed for it, on the off chance."

Mills drove from Brown Edge to Stockton Brook, finding the cottage on Brinkley Lane where Jane Trent was spending the night with her mother.

She opened the door nervously and peered out. Tyler offered his ID. "You've found something?" she asked. She looked like she'd been crying.

"We'd like to ask you a few questions," said Tyler.

In the cottage a fire roared in the hearth, and Trent offered the detectives a seat in the chairs opposite. The temperature in the room was oppressive.

"My mother," said Trent, as though apologising, "she feels the cold. She's just gone up to bed. The fire will start to die down now."

Tyler cut to it. "I would like to know where your husband was on the night Stacey was killed."

The look of incomprehension on her face was startling, and her mouth opened and closed without letting out any words. Then: "I ... I don't understand."

Tyler looked at her, watching the thoughts swirling, reflecting in the wild movements in her eyes. "Paul? We – I was at home, we were at home that night."

"He didn't go out at all during the evening, or later?"

"No, we were in all evening, we went to bed. What – what are you trying to say?"

"I understand that you have left your husband," said Tyler.

"You've been to see him, then? Where is he – have you arrested him?"

"What might we arrest him for, Mrs Trent?"

234

"You – you don't think ..? No, he's a bastard, I'm sick of the sight of him, but no, not that. I was with him all night."

"Are you aware that someone contacted your husband, to extract money?"

She eyed the detectives. "Stacey contacted him for money, apparently. But I thought he told you about that."

"I don't mean Stacey, Mrs Trent. Who else contacted your husband about money?"

"I really have no idea."

"You are not aware that your husband was being blackmailed?"

"Blackmailed about what? I don't understand what you're saying. What's he done?"

She looked from Tyler to Mills and back again, as though trying to dig out a clue as to what they were saying, and where this was going.

"Why are you leaving your husband?" asked Tyler.

"Does it need explaining? You've seen him, you've seen what he's like, the overbearing, arrogant ...

"I've stayed with him, I've remained in that house in the hope that one day Stacey might come back to us. That I would be there when she did; that we might play happy families once again."

"Happy families?" said Tyler.

"Something like that, yes."

"Did something happen, Mrs Trent?"

A voice sounded from upstairs. "Jane, is everything alright?"

She got up from the chair and walked to the foot of the stairs. "It's okay, mum, everything's fine."

"I heard voices down there. Are you sure everything's alright?"

"Mum, it's okay, you need to rest now, go to sleep."

"Is it Paul?"

"Mum, please go to sleep."

"If you're sure everything's alright. Goodnight, then."

"Goodnight, Mum."

Trent came back into the room. "You asked if something happened. Well, you tell me."

She found her chair and almost fell back into it.

"He was the doting father; there was never any question of that. I hardly got a look in. He couldn't stand other people having time with his precious daughter. I always had my suspicions, but he's a clever bastard, always has been. Stacey never said anything, but I saw changes along the way, and in my dark days those suspicions grew. And I tried to question them, contain them. Paul was good at dismissing my suspicions, of subtly insinuating paranoia. So I took the tablets and concentrated on my career, and I put my fears down to my own neurosis."

She looked at Tyler. "And someone found out and was blackmailing him? Stacey – was she threatening to tell me the truth?"

"We don't know that," said Tyler.

"No, you won't do," she said. "Because Paul's too bloody clever. Pity the poor blackmailer who tries to take *his* money! He blames her boyfriends for the way she turned out, and all the time it's festered at the back of my mind ... that the damage was done long before boyfriends came on the scene."

CHAPTER FORTY FOUR

"I'm not sure it takes us any closer to nailing who killed her," said Tyler, as Mills drove back to Cedar Lane. "No evidence that anyone was blackmailing – or *trying to blackmail* - Paul Trent. The same combinations are there to speculate on; nothing's changed at all. We've uncovered another level of filth, and that's about the extent of it."

Mills didn't argue. When they had returned to base he checked his messages and found one of interest. "Another one to cross off the list, sir," he said.

"What's that?"

"The mystery of Kev is a mystery no longer. Seeing as you refused permission for me to travel to Ibiza, I've had to let my fingers do the walking. Kev Blake is no more."

"You mean he's died or merely changed his name?"

"Never made it on the music scene; returned from the hippy trail to become a full time heroin addict. Died earlier this year; they found his body in a squat down in Islington."

"Nice part of the world," said Tyler.

After the DCI had finished updating his report he took it through and placed it ceremoniously on Carstairs' desk. Decisions would be forthcoming tomorrow, no doubt, or later in the week, depending on how the cookie crumbled. Perhaps Trent's solicitors would be the ones to drive the final nails into the coffin of his career.

Mills had reached a dead end and checked his watch. There didn't appear to be anything else to follow up that wouldn't wait until the morning. He yawned, catching Tyler's attention. "Get yourself home, Danny. Anything nice planned for what remains of your evening?"

"I'd planned a quiet night at home with the wife and kids," he said.

"Apologies for detaining you."

Mills hesitated for a moment. Tyler caught the look. "Go on, then. Say it, for old times' sake."

"Jim, look, are you alright?"

"Like I told you, and like I keep on telling you, I've rarely felt better. Pity there's nothing concrete to nail Trent for what he did all those years ago, but you can't win them all. At least his wife's finally free of him, but doubtless it's poor consolation."

"But you're sure *you're* okay, Jim?"

"Don't waste your time worrying over me."

"It's just - it's hard to tell with you sometimes."

"Take my word, will you? Anyway, I should be asking how things are with you."

"How do you mean?"

"I haven't seen you go near a pie or a biscuit for days now. I'm wondering whether ..."

"Yes?"

"Is there something you're not telling me?"

"How do you mean? What sort of thing?"

"I know you had a doctor's appointment recently."

"Oh, that: it was just a 'Well Man' thing. That's why I'm off the pies and pints and just about everything else that makes life worth living."

"Then ... is there something else you're not telling me?"

Mills eyed the DCI.

"If you're not ill, then I wonder if all of these visits to the local brothels lately haven't proved to be your undoing. You're looking trimmer and fitter than I've ever seen you. I'd even say that you've been working out. Not trying to attract a younger audience, by any chance?"

Mills was about to say something when Tyler burst out laughing.

"You have to excuse me. I haven't laughed in weeks. I'm sorry it had to be at your expense."

"Don't mention it. I'm happy to be of some service. While we're on the subject, my wife said I should ask about joining you on one of your runs. I wondered if she'd taken out a new life insurance policy on me."

"We could build you up slowly," said Tyler.

"You mean it?"

"I've grown sick of running myself into the ground. I'm making an effort to lighten up. We both appear to be looking across the desk at new men, Danny; at new versions of ourselves. You, I suspect, have your wife to thank, while my rebirth has come from an unexpected source."

"Anyone I know?" asked Mills.

"Chief Superintendent Carstairs."

"*Carstairs?*" Mills appeared baffled, and then his expression changed as though he was bracing himself for the inevitable pay off.

"I'm serious, Danny. That pompous oaf has opened my eyes."

Tyler's phone was ringing. He picked up, switchboard putting through an urgent call from *West End Girls*. Hayley Greener.

Ending the call he looked back across at Mills. "It seems you may have to cancel the remains of your evening," he said.

"What is it?"

"Get your coat. It looks as though events have taken a turn."

CHAPTER FORTY FIVE

Tyler explained in the car while Mills drove.

"Ron Hately turned up; his fifth visit of the day, apparently."

"I was there on one of his earlier visits," said Mills. "He didn't stay. He asked for Scarlet, like he always does, and then went home."

"Well, he wasn't giving it up," said Tyler. "And this last time, visit number five, when he was told Scarlet wasn't there he saw one of the other girls."

"Which one?" asked Mills. "There can't be many left there now."

"It was Lillistock. She's seen him before."

"Has something happened?"

"Rayworth was in the next room. The walls are quite thin, and she overheard something." While Tyler explained, Mills headed down through Shelton, into Stoke, eventually picking up London Road. "Hately was crying, really bawling, and Rayworth had just finished with a client and was apologising for the antics coming through the walls. The crying went on for some time, and she was wondering whether she ought to look in, to check everything was okay. Then she heard Hately start talking, saying he was sorry about Scarlet, about what happened. And here's the thing ..."

Mills was approaching the West End. "Rayworth heard him say: '*Scarlet shouldn't have done that. She knew how much I loved her. She was mine.*' Hately kept repeating it. So Rayworth went and told Greener, and here we are."

Mills swung in and pulled up outside *West End Girls*. Greener was at the door before they'd got out of the car. She met them out on the street. "Thank God you're here. There've been developments."

When Rayworth told Greener what she'd heard, the proprietor went up to the room occupied by Hately and Lillistock. But all was silent up there, and Greener had tapped on the door. "Everything alright in there?" But still no sound issuing. "May, is everything okay?"

"We're alright, so leave us alone." Hately's voice.

Greener knocking again. "*May?*"

"I said leave us alone will you."

Greener starting to turn the door handle, and Hately's voice, shouting now, blasting out in anger, "Stay out! I don't want to have to do something."

Greener looked shaken as she told all this to the detectives.

"You didn't hear May's voice?" asked Tyler.

"No, I didn't. Christ, I hope she's – that he hasn't ..."

Rayworth was back in the adjoining room, where the detectives joined her. "Heard anything more?" whispered Tyler.

"He was talking. His voice was low," said Rayworth. "I could hear him but I couldn't tell what he was saying."

"Did you hear any other voice?"

"I heard May, so at least he hasn't done her in, not yet. But he must be holding her. I mean, otherwise she'd just come out, wouldn't she? But she's still in there."

Tyler went out into the corridor and stood by the door. He knocked gently. "Roy?"

"Go away, I've told you. I don't want to hurt anyone. What have they done with Scarlet? I can't find her – she's not in here. There's just this other tart pretending to be my Scarlet."

242

"I'm here to help you, Roy."

"I don't need your help. I want to find Scarlet." Everything went quiet. Then the sound of gentle sobbing followed, and a voice so quiet that Tyler could just about hear it. "She shouldn't have done it. It hurts, Scarlet, you shouldn't have done it, you shouldn't have done this to me, you shouldn't have done it. You know how much you mean to me, you know that, and you know what you did, why did you do it, Scarlet? You shouldn't have done it you just shouldn't have done it." His voice was rising now, into a swell of agitation.

"Shouldn't have done what, Roy?"

"She shouldn't have gone with him! She was mine; she knew how much I loved her!" He was shouting, and the snarl in his voice was ugly.

"Please, Roy, open the door and we can talk about it."

Silence.

"Roy? Roy, please open the door."

A softer, gentler voice now: "I don't trust them. They tell you anything."

"Who does, Roy?"

"The ones here, they mislead you, they think they're being clever, but they're not clever at all. I know what's going on."

"What do they tell you, Roy?"

"They tell you things. They tell you Scarlet's dead."

Tyler could hear him crying.

"May," said Tyler.

"I'm here."

Her voice sounded timid, tinged with fear that she was plainly attempting to contain.

"Who are you talking to?" Hately's voice again.

"He's holding me, on the bed. He has a knife."

"I've asked who you're talking to!"

A stifled scream.

"It's alright, Mr Hately, *Roy*," said Tyler. "Nobody's going to hurt you. Nobody needs to get hurt. I'm here to help you, Roy."

"Go away and leave us alone in peace, will you."

Tyler went next door, walked to the window and looked out on the back of the building. To Rayworth he whispered, "You have access?"

"The gate round the side, yes."

"All rooms single glazed like this one?"

"I think so."

"Is there a rear exit?"

"No, it's boarded up. You can only get round the side. It's padlocked, but Hayley's got a key."

He gestured to Mills to follow him, and the detectives hurried down the stairs and along the corridor, getting the key from Greener, Tyler radioing for urgent back up, then out onto the street, and round to the side, unlocking the padlock and swinging the gate open. Rayworth was standing at the far window, the sash opened. "He's crying again," she whispered down.

Tyler looked around and found a half brick amongst the rubble. He stopped for a moment, and then handed it to Mills. "Give me one minute, and then smash the window." Mills looked at him but said nothing. "Don't worry, I'm not asking for heroics, Danny. I want you to cause a distraction, nothing more than that."

"But -"

"*One minute*," repeated Tyler, and then he was gone, back into the building, taking the stairs two at a time, waiting outside the door, his ear pressed to it.

He could hear Hately crying, muttering something intermittently between the sobs, words that the DCI couldn't quite catch. Standing poised, he waited, the seconds ticking inside his head like rockets going off, the tightness across his chest like a band of constricting iron, adrenalin pumping. And then the crash, the window going through, and Tyler was plunging through the doorway and into the room; in a split second he saw Hately turn back from the window, disorientated by the explosion of glass and now this rude entry from the doorway.

He was on the bed, Lillistock next to him, and in that moment she saw her chance and took it, leaping up, running from the room, Hately reaching back for her, but too late, she was gone.

The Stanley knife in his hand, Hately made to stand up, lashing out wildly as he did so; as the knife arced past Tyler was on him, wrestling the knife from his grip, Mills coming into the room now. But Hately wasn't giving up, he was stronger than Tyler could have imagined, and as the knife fell to the floor he lashed a fist out, catching the DCI and sending him down across the floor, dazed, blinking bright lights, Mills kicking the knife across the room before Hately could retrieve it.

And in the last moments before the room filled up with police officers as the backup finally arrived, it was Mills who threw himself on the back of Hately, pinning him to the ground as the man's hand reached in vain to retrieve the knife. A groggy Tyler revived himself and read Hately his rights. As the officers took him away, Mills looked at the DCI with concern. "You alright, Jim?"

"How many times are you going to ask me that stupid -"

And then his eyes rolled back into his head and he hit the ground with a crash.

CHAPTER FORTY SIX

Tyler was climbing out of a hole, lights glowing in the far distance. Sounds alien to him were swirling, not making any sense, utterly unfamiliar. He could hear drumming beyond the immediate sounds, and recognised his heartbeat, fading down to zero first and then picking up pace. He could see a dark figure standing in a corridor of light, a side-burned monster glistening with sweat and brandishing a stick. "You're for it, Tyler, we've found you out and we're going to roast you alive. You're going to wish that you'd never been born, boy!"

And then it came, the sound of laughter, like water falling onto a fire, quenching the flames, the sound growing, coming from the frail figure of a child, and growing to the stature of a man, the cacophony deafening, and the monster diminishing in the face of it, falling away into nothing at all.

He held the figure in the palm of his hand, watched it impotently swinging the stick at thin air, watched it dance in a frenzy as he poured laughter upon it, the monster assuming a thousand faces, and among them, after the hideous beasts of his youth and the tyrants he had faced and defeated during his time on the force in London, finally the face of CS Carstairs dissolving in the last volley of laughter.

"Jim ..."

"Who's there?"

"*Jim* ..."

A mirage, thought Tyler, a trick of the mind. He could see a large moustache looming over him; and then the rest of the face hiding behind it came into focus.

"Well, well, here's a thing, one in, one out!"

Tyler sat up. "How are you doing?"

"Better than you I'd say, by the look of things. That's some bruise you've got there," said Berkins, pointing to the side of Tyler's head.

"I'm okay. Bit woozy, that's all. They've mended you, then?"

"I'm good to go, Jim. I'm on my way home. They told me you were here so I thought I'd pop by. You have a story to tell me?"

"Something like that," said Tyler. "But it can wait."

"I look forward to hearing it. I'm hoping to start back next week, so a catch up is going straight in my diary as soon as I get back."

Mills called at the hospital later, and Tyler was already pestering the doctors to discharge him. "You know what it's like," he said to Mills. "The guardians of bureaucracy hold sway – the perpetual, eternal wait for paperwork, in their job and ours. The system rules the roost, and we are merely its servants."

"Nice speech," said Mills. "Sounds to me like concussion talking."

"Not lost your sense of humour in my absence, I see."

"They say it makes the heart grow fonder," said Mills. "Nice war wound, Jim. It will impress all the ladies for sure."

"I wonder which ladies we're talking about. But thank you. They can hardly discipline a man with a bruise on his head the size of an old man's fist."

"He was a strong old buzzard, Hately, more to him than you'd think. Took a few of us to get him out of that place I can tell you. He was screaming to call up the dead, and still demanding to see Scarlet and asking what we'd done with her. And now we can't get a word out of him."

"Psychiatric assessment?"

"It's underway – and well overdue."

"On the assumption that I still have a job, I'll be back for the formal interviews. I saw Berkins earlier. He's expecting to return to his post imminently; the man's a legend. So it looks like Carstairs will have to look elsewhere for fresh meat."

"Can't say I'm sorry to see the back of him," said Mills. "The way he looks down his nose, it's like he can't help himself."

"Takes rigorous training to achieve that," said Tyler. "There's worse than Carstairs, believe me, but I could hear the knives sharpening the day he arrived. He'd have loved to add my scalp to his collection. It's mandatory to have a few on your wall when you're striving for the upper echelons of our sacred department."

He looked at Mills with admiration. "I must say, you cut a fine figure these days, Danny."

"If I knew you were going to take the piss I'd have saved myself the trouble."

"You see how it is? Everywhere I turn I find myself misunderstood. No, I'm serious. And we'll organise that run sometime soon."

"You really don't have to, Jim."

"See that you hold me to it, and I'll do the same."

CHAPTER FORTY SEVEN

Roy Hately sat next to his solicitor in the interview room at Cedar Lane. Tyler and Mills sat facing him, a desk between them.

Mills observed how calm Hately looked. He had been screaming and flailing like a mad thing back at *West End Girls*, and leaving one officer with a smashed lip and another with a black eye, aside from the bash on the temple that he had delivered to the DCI.

There appeared to be no attempt at deceit, as far as could be discerned, with long stretches of confusion mixing in with moments of lucidity, and at times almost startling clarity. An old man with escalating dementia, no doubt compounded by the emotional stress, the acute grief, caused by the death of his wife.

The days had become a blur for Hately. There was no point in using terms like 'Sunday evening', as they appeared to have no reference point for him anymore. Mills asked him about Scarlet. He looked down at the ground, as though he hadn't heard, or else didn't wish to acknowledge the question. But when Mills asked him again, he looked up and issued a glowing smile. "I know Scarlet. How's she doing? I'm hoping to see her again later. We belong together, you know. I love her, don't you know that?"

"What happened to Scarlet?" asked Mills.

"Nobody will tell me. I keep going there and asking but they won't tell me. There's other girls live there, and some of them are nice to me, talk to me, you know. But it's not the same. There's no-one quite like my Scarlet."

"What was so special about her?" asked Tyler.

Hately was still looking at Mills, as though an act of ventriloquy had allowed the DS to ask the question without moving his lips.

"Mr Hately, what was so special about Scarlet," repeated Tyler. And this time Hately's gaze shifted over in the direction of the DCI.

"What was so special?" Hately's smile appeared to glow fiercer, and then a faint mist came into his eyes, and he blinked. "How can I put it? I mean to say, it's love, isn't it. How do you describe, how can you explain something like that?"

"What happened, Mr Hately? What really happened to Scarlet?"

He looked for a few moments at Tyler, and then something in his gaze appeared to shift, a dull recognition. He said, "You mean ... *that night*?"

"Yes, that night. Tell me what happened."

"Oh, nothing much; she was at her usual place, you know, where the other girls live."

"You mean at *West End Girls*?"

"I think that's the one, down from my place. I'd seen her earlier, even asked her to marry me, and I knew she wanted to, I knew she could tell how much I loved her, how much I wanted to be with her. But she had to be somewhere, she said that, and I could tell she was lying to me." He looked puzzled suddenly. "I just didn't understand it."

"Didn't understand what, Mr Hately?" asked Tyler.

"How can you lie to someone when you love them, and want to be with them? How can you do that?" The first signs of agitation started to manifest. Mills could see the tightening in the man's demeanour and an edge creeping back into his voice. "I knew something was up

– wrong, you know. I knew she was going somewhere, and so I waited. I saw her leave with another of the girls who lived there, another one of the regulars. They started walking together but then they went separate ways."

"You followed her?"

"Followed ... how do you mean?"

"You followed Scarlet?"

"Oh, I see. Yes - what could I do? I had to know what was going on. If we loved one another and were going to be together, we had to know what was going on, didn't we."

Tyler let the man gather his thoughts, and then he asked, "Where did you follow her to?"

"Follow her to? I don't know that! We walked for miles. But I had to know, of course I did. It was some park, and as soon as we got there I knew what was going on. I thought, you're meeting some lad, that's what you're doing. You dirty filthy bitch!"

Hately seemed shaken by his sudden outburst. When he had regained his composure, he said, "They sat smoking and talking, and I watched them. I thought, what are you waiting for? I thought, if you're going to betray me, get on and do it."

The interview room was suddenly quiet, and to Mills it seemed that Hately was preparing himself, summoning reserves.

"Then it started. He had his trousers down and she had her dress up and they were going at it ... and she was making all these noises, like she'd never done it before, like she was saying to me, this is how it should be done, this is what I want."

The tears were running down his face, and he looked pleadingly at Tyler. "Don't you see, Mister, it's like she was scorning me, like she was telling me that she had found her true lover and had no need for me now."

He was crying, and squeezing hard at the tops of his legs with both his hands, his fingers tightened like claws, digging through the fabric of his clothing, down to the flesh beneath.

The solicitor started to speak, but Tyler waved him down.

"He showed his colours, his true colours, he did," said Hately, his teeth gritted now. "He scarpered and left her there, all alone she was. I went to comfort her, to tell her it was alright."

Hately fell silent again.

"But that isn't what happened, is it?" said Tyler. "You didn't comfort her, did you?"

"I tried to."

"Why did you take a knife with you?"

A look of confusion came over him. "The knife, yes, I took that. I knew there was going to be trouble, see. When I set out, I knew she going to see someone, and I had to defend her, didn't I? Who else was going to look out for her? A young woman going out alone like that, late at night, and there's people around these days you wouldn't trust around young girls. So I took a knife with me, the one I keep for cutting carpets and things like that. It was in my old tool box. I don't use my tools anymore, not really, not since I retired."

He was starting to ramble. Tyler said, "After the young man left her alone, you say that you went over to Scarlet?"

"I went over to her, yes."

"Were you angry with her?"

"Was I angry? Wouldn't you be angry? She tells me she loves me and then she's off doing that with some boy in a park! I wanted to teach her a lesson, that's what I wanted to do. I wanted to let her know that there are consequences when you tell someone you love them. You don't lead people on down garden paths – you don't say things like that lightly. People have to learn – I say it's all about commitment."

"What happened?" asked Tyler.

"She looked at me like I was some monster coming out of the trees. It's like she didn't even recognise me. I said, 'It's me, your Roy!' But she was starting to scream and so I ran to her to stop her doing that and I only put my hand over her mouth - but she was fighting, pushing me away, lashing out at me - and the filthy language she was using ..."

Mills could picture the scene. The woman sitting there smoking in the peace of a late Sunday night at the lido, and suddenly there's Hately approaching her, a knife in his hand.

Hately jumped to his feet, his gaze trained on the far wall of the interview room, as though watching the scene unfolding on a screen, his eyes bulging in an aspect of horror at what he was seeing. "No, it wasn't meant to be like that. I must have caught her - across the throat, no, I didn't mean to, I'd never hurt her - and when I saw the blood, well, what can you do, what could I do, I panicked – well, you would, wouldn't you. I didn't know what to do. I was looking down on that beautiful face, on her beautiful face, and I watched it grow ugly, it was ugly with deceit and treachery and betrayal and call it what you like but I couldn't stand looking at it and she was nothing but meat on a slab and I took the knife to it ..."

CHAPTER FORTY EIGHT

Hately was charged with the murder of Stacey Trent. His lucid account of what transpired at the lido showed beyond doubt that he must have been there. The knife matched as the credible murder weapon. There was no doubt at all in the minds of the detectives.

Mills sat watching Tyler, who was looking troubled. "It was right under our noses, Danny. The problem being, I was determined to look elsewhere."

"I wouldn't beat yourself up," said Mills, wondering why he was even bothering to say it. Tyler was the world champ at beating himself up.

Tyler was about to speak, when Mills took a call. The call was brief and after it ended Mills said, "May Lillistock."

"What about her?"

"She's just come into the station. She wants to speak to you."

"Interesting," said Tyler. "I wonder what she wants."

"Perhaps she wants to pin a medal on you for saving her life."

"You think so?"

"Only one way to find out, sir."

Tyler got to his feet and for a moment looked unsteady.

"You alright ..?" started Mills, and then waved a hand to retract the question. "Silly of me to ask," he said.

"I'll let it go this time," said Tyler. "I stood up too quickly. The excitement gets the better of me some days and causes a rush of blood to the head."

Mills nodded. "I tell you what, though," he said.

"Tell me."

"You haven't half killed Carstairs' pig."

"That's a rather curious turn of phrase."

"To put it another way: he's like a bear with a sore head this morning."

"I know the feeling," said Tyler, touching at his temple. "But he can hardly hang the local hero out to dry, can he? I imagine he's busy clearing out his desk ready for the return of the mighty Berkins."

"I can't wait," said Mills.

"Neither can Berkins. There's a man who thrives on his work, God help him. Never one to swing the lead."

"Hately," said Mills, shaking his head. "It's a sad case really. He's now saying he's never heard of anyone called Scarlet. Hasn't a clue where that knife came from, never seen it before. And last night he was heard calling out her name in his sleep."

"It's a sad one alright. But murder cases generally are." With that he turned to go, and then immediately turned back. "Actually, Danny, maybe you ought to come down with me."

"So I can watch with pride when she pins that medal for bravery to your chest?"

"Why else?"

They took her through to an interview room. "Cup of tea?" asked Tyler, but Lillistock declined. She was dressed in black jeans and a peach top, but it wasn't her clothing that stood out. She had a different look about her, one that Tyler hadn't seen before. There had always been a touch of arrogance, of swagger, even, he had thought, yet it seemed to have been replaced now with one of stark humility. Looks, though, he knew could often prove to be deceptive.

"How can I help you?" he asked.

She swallowed hard, an anxious look pervading. "First," she said, "I'd like to thank you, for what you did."

"I was doing my job," said Tyler. "You don't have to thank me."

"I don't know what Hately would have done. I was sure he was going to kill me. I sat with him once before, but he was never like that. I wondered if it was something I said, some trigger that set him off."

"It wasn't your fault."

"But I might have said something, pressed a button or -"

"He had the knife with him," said Tyler. "So unless he was in the habit of carrying it around, I suspect that he was bent on trouble. I don't think it was anything you did or said that caused him to do what he did. It could have been anyone in that room, you were just unlucky."

"Well, thank you, anyway," she said.

Her eyes remained on Tyler. "Was there something else?" he asked her.

Again the hard swallow and the accompanying look of fear. "Actually, yes, there is. I ... have a confession to make."

Tyler allowed her the time to frame whatever it was that was on her mind. It took her a few moments to prepare herself. At last she said, "I wasn't exactly straight with you."

"About what?"

"I ..."

"Take your time," he said.

"I knew Dean Stewart."

"I'm not aware that's a crime in itself," said Tyler, catching Mills' eye as he said it. "But do go on."

"Maybe it doesn't make any difference now. But I want to be straight with you. I feel I owed it to you, for what you've done. You see, we talked about Stacey, about her being, you know, about her having rich parents."

The words were coming out hard.

"You mean that you and Stewart ..." started Tyler.

"I keep my eyes and ears open. I see and I hear a lot of things, doing what I do, working at those places. And I found out that Stacey was trying to get money out of a lecturer she reckoned had molested her, or had an affair with her, or whatever it was. I knew Kelly was involved in that, and that he was knocking about with her. And the thing is ..."

She couldn't seem to quite bring herself to say it. Tyler urged her again to take her time, and then she was taking a tissue out of her bag and blotting her eyes with it.

"I told Dean about it. I told him about Stacey going after the teacher for money. That she was going to college but the reason she was going was to fleece the teacher."

"And what was Stewart's response?" asked Tyler.

"He was angry. He reckoned she was always messing him about and this was another example of her not being straight with him. He said he was sick of always being the last to know and that he was going to teach her a lesson."

"What kind of lesson?"

"He said she was messing about going after some lousy letch when there was a pot of gold sitting right behind her own front door."

258

"He was referring to her parents?"

"Dean – he planned to threaten to tell her parents, tell them about why she had left college, and how she was trying to blackmail her teacher. That it was time she had a taste of her own medicine. He was going to ask for money – his settlement, he called it. She'd have to pay him off or else he'd make the call to her parents and let them know exactly what a scumbag they had for a daughter."

Lillistock let out the tears, and then she said, "You know, with what happened to Stacey, I wondered if it had anything to do with that. You know: Kelly, or even Stewart. But I couldn't see Dean hurting anyone like that; he was always the gentlest person you could imagine. He's alright, really, he is, but Stacey, well, she had hurt him, and he wanted to hit back. I'm not even sure it was about the money. I think he just wanted to hurt her in some way, and get his, as he saw it, compensation. And ..."

"Yes?"

"I'm ashamed to say, he offered to give me a slice of the money when he got it. Said it would help buy me out of this life I was living. And I wanted to get out, and I have done. But I didn't need any money from Stacey's parents or from Dean Stewart. He kept calling round to see me. I felt sorry for him. Anyway, it's all done with now, and I'm out of that life. Some last shift, though."

"It certainly was," said Tyler.

"I couldn't tell you or anyone about it; I thought - I was scared that it might look like me or Dean had a reason for killing Stacey. But he would never have done that, I see that now. I'm sorry I didn't tell you the truth."

Tyler listened, and then he said, "And I'd like to make my own apology."

Mills coughed, as though to signal that enough had been said. But even as he made the gesture he knew that his efforts would once again prove to be wasted.

"I made the suggestion that you do some extra shifts, and you rightly made a complaint against me. I knew that you and Stewart weren't telling me everything, and I pushed too hard to force the issue. I was wrong to do that."

Lillistock beamed a smile at the DCI. "I never heard a police officer talk like that before."

"You won't have done," barked up Mills. "It only happens here."

She laughed and looked again at Tyler. "Perhaps," she said, "we can call it quits."

CHAPTER FORTY NINE

"Seems your instincts weren't so far off the mark after all," said Mills as they headed back up to the office. "A little off beam, but nothing that some fine tuning ..."

Tyler turned to him, his eyebrows raised.

"*Sir*," Mills added.

Tyler grinned. "Just don't let the likes of Carstairs hear you lambasting a senior officer like that, do you hear, DS Mills?"

"Loud and clear!"

"And ... talk of the devil."

Carstairs was standing at the top of the stairs, appearing to look down on the two detectives from a great height. "A word," he said, looking at Tyler. "My office."

*

"It would seem things have somewhat resolved after all, despite your best efforts," said Carstairs.

Tyler frowned at the obscure phrasing of the barbed sentence. "If you mean, we got a result, then I'd have to agree."

A look of disdain was fired back across the desk at him, but Tyler soaked it up without blinking.

"Mistakes were made, and you attracted complaints that could have been avoided; but top of it all, why the hell did you feel the need to ask a sex worker to do extra shifts? I mean, it beggars belief."

"An error of judgement," said Tyler.

"I'll say it was. Pressing buttons, seeing how far you could go – you're a police officer, a detective chief

261

inspector, no less, and therefore eminently answerable for your actions."

Tyler was beginning to wonder if the rant was set in for the day. Occasionally he couldn't account for his actions; occasionally they left him as baffled as those around him. Running on instinct was fine when things worked out, but it was close to impossible to explain the methods those instincts sometimes called upon when things were heading south.

Carstairs was still awaiting a response. Tyler couldn't think of a suitable one appropriate to the occasion. Flying once again by the seat of his pants, he opted for: "Desperate times call for desperate methods."

"What the hell is that supposed to mean?"

"I've really no idea," said Tyler.

*

A few days later, a familiar sight cast its lighter shadow in the CID office. CS Berkins was standing in the doorway, his moustache appearing resplendent as it shuffled beneath its owner's warm smile. A round of applause issued from the few occupants of the office, and Berkins responded with a cheerful, "Thank you. It's good to be back."

He led Tyler through to the chief superintendant's den and took a seat, before inviting him to sit opposite. "I really can't tell you how good it is to be here, Jim," he said.

"You don't need to tell me. I can see for myself."

"So, have I missed anything?"

Tyler stifled a grin. "Not much, just a routine murder investigation."

He caught the twinkle in Berkins' eye. "I hear some excellent work was done, if not entirely appreciated. How did you find our friend?"

Tyler fished a tissue from his pocket and dabbed at his eyes. "The first few weeks will be the worst, but I'll get over it ... eventually ... given time. I miss him terribly. We have so much in common."

"Good work, Jim."

"Thank you."

CHAPTER FIFTY

Tyler sat in the car looking up at the flat. A light was burning in the window, beckoning. He'd taken the call earlier and he'd been chewing over it since.

May Lillistock.

It hadn't worked out with Stewart, not in any sense of the word, apparently. But with a new career, a fresh start, she was moving on. Though there was still one item of business left unfinished.

Tyler thought over the facts of the case, the tangles, and the bitter ironies. He thought about Stewart wanting to hit back at Stacey Trent for messing him about, letting him down, two and three timing him. And Stewart thought he was onto something with that half-baked notion of blackmail, if that wasn't an altogether too strong a word for what he had in mind. *Compensation*, that's the word Lillistock had used. And it didn't sound too far off the mark.

If Stewart had know the half of it; if he had known the far darker truth of what lay behind the damaged girl that he had once fallen in love with, no matter how briefly. But what Trent had once chosen to divulge to Wormsley, she had not chosen to place into the keeping of Stewart, or anyone else. And Wormsley had proven a poor choice of keeper, a woeful confessor despite his gleaming credentials once upon a time.

As for Paul Trent, well, it had cost him his marriage, and the life of his daughter; if the man was human, the suffering would be endless and might even prove to be justice enough. Who could tell? Who could fully comprehend the delicate balances of the genuine scales of real justice? It wasn't in the gift of Tyler, or anyone else, to ultimately decide on those matters.

His mind moved back to the conversation earlier, over the phone: Lillistock calling out of the blue, telling him that if she was barking up the wrong tree to then simply disregard her as another crank in what for him had likely been a week chocked full with them.

Yet he hadn't been able to disregard her.

"Perhaps I was picking up the wrong signals," she said. "And it wouldn't be the first time and doubtless it won't be the last."

There was no ethical dilemma that he could see, and none that he cared to allow to hold sway. A woman he had come across over the course of his investigations; a case now closed; nothing to be compromised; nothing that might confuse his professional judgement in any way. Whichever way he turned it, he was clear.

He looked across at the flat, that burning light with its promise of *possibilities*. The lonely life, did it suit him? How many times would he have to ask himself that same question, and fail to satisfy with an answer? His hand was on the car door, and then it was back on the steering wheel. He watched himself getting out of the car, walking towards the flats, and then he watched himself putting the car into gear and driving away, back into the night.

The minutes ticked by. And all the time the light in the window shone brightly, asking its question.

CHAPTER FIFTY ONE

Mills spent the evening at home with his wife and children, and after the kids had gone to bed he felt whacked. "I think I'm going to turn in," he said.

"What a good idea," said his wife. "It's been a stressful time. I'll be up myself in a few minutes."

He got undressed and climbed into bed, and not long after his wife joined him.

"So, they all lived happily ever after," she said. "Berkins back at the helm, Tyler still in a job and no after effects from that bang on the head, the killer behind bars, and the detective's instincts finally proven to have been in the right ball park."

"That's about the shape of it," said Mills. "Though I sincerely hope that at least one person I could mention doesn't live happily ever after."

"He has a divorce to look forward to. I imagine he's going to find it an expensive experience, so at the very least there's pain coming to his pocket."

"We live in hope and gather in small mercies."

"Well, Danny Mills, as I live and breathe - you poet you!"

"Something I remember from my schooldays. But I've no idea who said it."

"Did you have to ruin the moment?"

"Sorry."

His wife smiled at him. "So, only one thing left unresolved, then."

"What's that?"

"What happened to the woman Tyler was seeing?"

"I told you, she moved down to London."

"It's an hour or so on the train, Danny."

"I didn't like to ask any more."

"You're a typical man, do you know that?"

"It has been said before."

"You're all bloody useless when it comes to the important things in life."

"Oh, I don't know about that," said Mills.

"Go on, then, what have you got?"

"I do believe that there might be another iron in the fire."

"I'm intrigued."

"I thought you might be. And so am I."

"Come on, then, who is it?"

"I might be on the wrong track entirely."

"Danny!" She punched him on the arm.

"I thought I'd done with violence for one week."

"There's more where that came from."

"Well, Jim took a call as I was leaving. I didn't catch who the caller was, but putting my considerable, my near-legendary detective skills to use – and stretching them to the very limits ..."

Mills' wife looked at her watch.

"There was something about the way Jim took that call. It reminded me of ..."

"Do you plan to spin this out all night?"

"I think he was talking to someone we recently entertained in the interview room. I could see the way she was looking at him then and I knew there was something brewing."

"You mean -"

"That's exactly who I mean."

"But I thought she was with that other guy, that whatisname ..?"

267

"You really ought to keep up when I'm telling you confidential information pertaining to highly classified - "

"Yes, yes!"

"You mean Stewart."

"That's the one. What's he think about the police officer who's been hounding him running off with his latest girlfriend?"

Mills dropped his voice to a stage whisper. "Okay, I'm messing, I'll tell you the truth. She came back into the station, asked to see Jim again. The way he told it, she said to him that one good turn deserved another. That he'd made one outrageous suggestion to her, and now she wished to return the favour."

"She asked him out – what, using one of the interview rooms?"

"He said he was too stunned to refuse. Of course, and not for the first time, he asked about Stewart. And you know what she said?"

"What did she say?"

"That she'd had enough of boys and wanted a real man."

Mills couldn't hold it any longer and cracked up laughing, his wife punching him on the arm again. He cried out in mock pain. "Sometimes Danny I don't know when you're winding me up."

"And that," he said, "is the way I like it."

*

On his day off he drove into the city and up the hill to the ancient village, parking up on Penkhull Terrace. Tyler was already in his running gear when he opened the door to greet him.

"Are you sure you want to do this?" he said as Mills climbed out of the car, wheezing a little as he did so, and sporting a pair of cord trousers that he used for painting, and an old work shirt with the arms cut off.

"Are *you* sure, Jim?"

"I'll be gentle with you, Danny."

"I bet you say that to all the overweight and under exercised police officers."

"Another of my failings, I'm afraid. The trouble with Penkull, as you are about to discover, it's on a hill; so what goes down must, at some point, struggle back up again, as I have found to my cost on many occasions. We could have chosen the beautiful landscape of your new country home."

"Not a chance," said Mills. "I was raised in the city and I will die of exhaustion in the city."

"Spoken like a trooper. Shall we?"

Avoiding the gruelling inclines descending in the directions of Stoke and the West End, they set off instead towards the gentler slopes of Hartshill, finding a pace at first unnatural to them both, and then, to their mutual surprise, discovering, against all the odds, a rhythm that felt as natural as life itself.

The End

Author Note

Thank you for reading *Scarlet Ribbons*. I hope you enjoyed it. And thanks to Val Hackett, who raised a considerable sum of money for the Born Free charity bidding to have her name used in one of my books. The real Val is a tireless worker for this wonderful charity, and I hope she likes what I have done with her name. Thanks also to all the usual suspects for reading earlier drafts of the book and offering encouragement and helpful suggestions along the way.

Not for the first time in the present series, I have taken liberties with the geography of North Staffordshire, for the purpose of telling a good story. I hope that residents of the affected areas are not unduly concerned.

Printed in Great Britain
by Amazon

22363268R00158